There was a flash of
brilliant white light and at
that moment time seemed
to stand still.

The memories of many lifetimes
cascaded through his consciousness,
startling him with their clarity and profusion.
In awe he realised that there was no room
for fear, only love.

He was safe and warm and above all else
he was free.

Free in a way he would never
have believed possible.

Coming Soon from David Mercer

Jordanis
The Grave Diggers
Screaming Souls

STILLBORN

By

David Mercer

SHARK BOOKS

BODMIN
England

STILLBORN

Copyright ©1991 David Mercer

ISBN 1 898816 00 X

SHARK BOOKS
Published in Great Britain by Mistral Publishing Ltd
Bodmin PL31 1NG
Cornwall
U.K.

Cover Design by Mistral Publishing Ltd from original artwork by Patrick Gamble

Printed by Cox & Wyman Ltd Reading

For Bruno
A Real Friend

CHAPTER ONE

The doors of the casualty unit swung open as the gurney was pushed forward. The crash team were waiting, the casualty registrar moved forward immediately and was already checking vital signs even as the ambulancemen still pushed the stretcher into a small side ward.

As he made his own observations he questioned the breathless paramedic who moved in front, IV bag in his hand.

"BP just about gone, pupils dilated. He's not breathing ......How long?"

"10 to 12 minutes! I gave him mouth to mouth..heart massage..breathed on his own for a few seconds."

A nurse had connected a monitor. The heart beat was weak and erratic. She clamped a mask over the patient's face and the mechanical respirator took over.

The erratic beep of the monitor faltered.

"Straight line! Defib...100ml adrenaline!"

A syringe was passed quickly to the registrar. He wiped the sweat from his forehead then bent over and pushed the long needle into the man's heart. The nurse beside him held the pads of the defibrilator ready. The high voltage whistle indicated that the machine was charging.

Casting the now empty syringe aside he took hold of the pads, the whistling had stopped.

While the medical team were busy in their effort to save the patient, David Hawkin had waited patiently in the background. His own equipment was ready, checked and re-checked. More out of habit than necessity he checked his instruments once again. Then he walked over to his colleague who sat at the computer terminal.

He leant over and whispered into his ear.

"I think this is it Michael. Be ready, make sure the door is

closed properly, check the bias."
Michael Tamasoto stood up. As he moved away he placed a large hand on David's shoulder and squeezed.

"Stand Clear!"
A thud, the patient's body arched. The high frequency whistle as the defibrilator started recharging.
All eyes were on the monitor, the single pulse that accompanied the discharge trailed away.
Straight line.
The intern increased the voltage. The whistle stopped.
"Clear!"
Thwhomp.
Straight line.
Again.
Straight Line.
Again....
The registrar straightened, leaving the pads of the defibrilator on the body. The rest of the crash team looked at him. He was young although there were lines around his eyes from tiredness and experience. Death, although common place where he worked, was an adversary and was never surrendered to without a fight and much regret.
Again he wiped the sweat from his eyes and fore-head, then brushed his hair back with his hand. The action suggested he was about to do something else but instead of moving he just lifted his eyes to return the looks of the others. There was an expression there of reluctant surrender, of defeat. When he spoke there was a slight hoarseness.
"That's it! Thanks."
He turned to leave.
"Doctor?..."

He stopped and turned to find the speaker. It was the first time he had paid David Hawkin any attention since entering the room. Slowly, his eyes took in the two men and their array of equipment. His tired expression came alive as he answered.

"All yours.....Mr Hawkin." The emphasis on Mr, a sneer crept on to his face, the anger evoked at losing the battle of life had found a target. He turned and was about to leave but again David Hawkin's words stopped him in mid stride.

"You can't leave...the room is sealed. Could you ask your team to move away from the body please?"

The doctor shrugged and turned to his staff.

"Come on girls and boys...lets watch the show." His words were cold, sarcastic. He led them over to the little row of seats against the wall. They sat down and ignoring David and Michael began to talk among themselves.

"The thoracic injuries were very extensive....the spine was obviously damaged....

....Even if he had lived it wouldn't have been much of a life.

....How did it happen?...

...Explosion, five or six casualties but this poor bugger got the worst of it...

...that big chemical plant down by the docks."

The lights dimmed. The chatter subsided. Even with the apathy the medics felt towards David Hawkin's experiments, their attention was being caught. Perhaps their interest was only drawn by their wish to see failure. This was after all a threat to their own disciplines.

David was standing by the gurney placing his own monitors on to the corpse's head while Michael sat at the terminal, watching his instruments.

The clipped electronic voice of the computer reported. "....brain function ceased. No Alpha or Beta emissions detectable. Estimated time since brain death... Three minutes, thirty seconds and counting... thirty one..."

The room was still. The eerie half light and the electronic voice had combined to create an atmosphere that even the medical team could not ignore. David waited for that magical five minute barrier to be broken and as the seconds ticked by he reflected on how this had all come to be.

Until recently David Hawkin had been a Professor of Sciences at Cambridge University. When his time had not been taken up with teaching duties, he had always dedicated much of his free time to research. In some ways the lifestyle of a University professor was ideal for him, there was plenty of spare time and he had access to most of the facilities he needed.

Of course, when there was industrial backing in the way of research grants, then the resources could be enormous but industry wanted their pound of flesh too and wouldn't put their money behind a project that seemed to be too far off the mainstream or if they couldn't see a profit at the end of the day. The university, on the other hand, was a lot more open minded. It did not have a commercial axe to grind, it was after all a place of learning and its staff were there primarily to teach.

During his last few years at Cambridge David had taken full advantage of the facilities available.

His research was unusual, his chosen subject was 'death'. As part of his fact finding he had collected and analysed a lot of data on after death experiences, a phenomenon that seemed to be increasingly common as medical science improved its own ability to cheat death. Resuscitation techniques had improved dramatically allowing patients to be 'brought back' after longer and longer periods of apparent death. It was almost like the improving times of athletes to run the 1500 metres. Casualty doctors seemed to measure their success by their ability to cheat death. The barrier was being continually pushed back, seconds being added to the record for post death recovery.

Strangely it indicated a separate stage to death, a stage before brain cell damage when memory and character would be partially or wholly destroyed.

David had studied dozens of reports which all gave the same hard-line indications and from these results he theorised that at a time approximately five minutes after the moment of death, something either left the body or died. Something seemingly intangible, a component of living beings not previously identified.

It was of course an age old phenomena, a facet of our being that had been recognised for millennia by spiritualists and theologians of just about every persuasion. Strangely it had until now eluded the intense investigative powers of Western medical scientists and physicians. It would be surprising indeed, to find a reference to the spirit in any medical library.

The question he now sought the answer to was that if something left the body, where did it go? Did it simply die or did it continue to exist in another form? Elsewhere.

In a new life form perhaps?

He had published a paper on his findings. Much to

the ridicule of many of his colleagues he had embellished his findings with his own theories. His ideas had overstepped the boundaries of conventional science, incorporating theological arguments and supposition.

He had dared to give his paper a very non scientific and emotive heading.

'Reincarnation. Myth or a credible alternative to death?'

It was at this point that one of the multinational pharmaceutical companies, CDG, had stepped in to sponsor further research. To the chagrin of many of his colleagues he had been given a grant to carry out further research on his thesis.

This was his current project, to prove or disprove the concept of reincarnation. It was a contentious issue, one given little credence by mainstream scientists and physicians and also, in England at least, it challenged the beliefs of the Church.

Yet here he was in a specially prepared side ward at the casualty department of a prominent London Hospital, fully funded by CDG and receiving the reluctant co-operation of medical staff and the use of hospital facilities.

He looked across at Michael Tamasoto, his friend and colleague. David smiled.

He was lucky to have him as an assistant.

Michael's strength was as a biologist but he also had particular expertise with the use of computers in analysis and model projection.

After months of preparation he and Michael were finally carrying out the first human experiment. This was the moment when his theories and beliefs would be confirmed or when their efforts would end in failure.

David shivered, he knew that failure would be absolute. If he was wrong, they would be ridiculed. The path he had chosen was too unconventional for their professional credibility to survive. He was also aware that so far it was mostly theory and pretty wild theory at that.

He was understandably nervous.

As David watched the seconds ticking away he suddenly experienced an overwhelming surge of self-doubt. How had he allowed himself to jump to these conclusion? To be so outspoken about his beliefs? He was a scientist - he should have stuck to the facts, not allowed his ideas to wander like they had, from fact to something more like mythology!

In the beginning it had been all science, it was when there were gaps in his knowledge that some deeply repressed beliefs of his own had somehow sprung up to fill the voids. He had started with a little unusual data on this transition between life and death and had tried to develop a reasonable theory to explain this phenomenon. The truth too was that he had allowed some of his own feelings to prejudice his interpretation of this data, to steer his assumptions.

David was not a believer of any kind, too rebellious to allow his own ideas to fit into someone else's doctrine although at the same time any theological instincts he did possess may have leant towards Buddhism in a broad sense, to the idea of reincarnation. He wasn't a 'Psycho freak', didn't visit spiritualist churches or seek answers from Indian gurus. He considered himse!f logical and believed that he had his feet on the ground but he also trusted his feelings and it had been certain personal instincts that had almost unconsciously steered him to the tentative conclusions he had reached.

Seeds sown in childhood had not blossomed uncontrollably into realisation but had nagged, asking for answers.

David looked around the room in a daze. Vaguely he heard the mechanical voice counting down the seconds and it seemed as if it was enunciating the last moments of his life. The seconds ticked by and he had this sudden awful feeling that this was to be his Nemesis, what happened now would be eradicable and would decide his future, whether good or bad.

As he waited he thought back to his childhood, to the first seed that had fired his imagination and had inauspiciously begun the journey that had led him to this point. It had come from his grandmother, a staunch Methodist and the sort of person whose narrow Victorian outlook you would least expect to have prompted into being this obscure passion and this strange chain of events.

She had given him a book written by a Methodist preacher. It was a simple little book, divided into four stories, each a separate incarnation of the same two people who always met again in each life.

Why? It was a question he had asked himself many times. Why should a devout Methodist, an established writer in the early part of this century whose other works were mostly all whimsical looks at his society's middle class lives, why should he let his writings and his theological considerations wander

on to such a subject?...such a singular and dramatic
diversion from his other books, contrary to his own
strong religious beliefs and those that existed in his
day and that would be held by his peers?

Then there was something else.....his recurrent childhood nightmare. He couldn't remember when it
started, the nightmare seemed to be his first memory
but even now as an adult he could remember with
such clarity the fear he had experienced. In the dream,
he would always wake up screaming, night after night.
It was a dream that ended in him being held down
while a man cut off his leg with a very large saw.

The dream had faded as he grew up, probably the
last time he had experienced it had been when he was
five, in 1950. It was only recently when his thoughts
had been on the reincarnation project that he had
remembered the dream and had delved into his
memory to inspect it. The discovery he had made had
been quite unexpected.

He visualised the scene once again, he was held down
by others while this man was sawing his leg. He
remembered that when he had recently reviewed his
nightmare again after all those years, for the first time
since his childhood, his adult mind had recognised
things that had not been noticed by the child.

In those early days, David had been too young to read
and there was no television in his home, his experience of the world was limited. Even so, the adult had
suddenly recognised something important. The way
the people in his dream were dressed, in simple
clothing of long ago....like quakers or...seamen.

Then all the pieces had suddenly fitted together like
the pieces of a puzzle. Without the input from books
or film, how had he conjured up such a scene? Where

had it come from? He couldn't have imagined it, he was too young, he didn't know that hundreds of years earlier this had been how they would have removed a gangrenous leg. The only way he could have known these things was consciously, from his own memory, from a time before he was born.... An earlier life.

He had realised in an instant that this made sense. Nobody remembered earlier lives, our only pre-life memories seem to be character elements, ideas, attitudes; trapped in our genetic memories, passed down biologically by our parents. But if reincarnation did actually happen why couldn't we remember our earlier selves? Perhaps we were not supposed to, who knows what plans direct our lives, what destinies our spirit is supposed to follow. Are our earthly memories of any consequence or value? If our spiritual growth is the only important facet of our continuing reincarnation, then is it not better that our spirit in it's rebirth should be unfettered by mortal memory?

Or perhaps it is much simpler than that, just a safety valve to protect us from the trauma of death and rebirth?

As the pieces fell together the dream had made sense to David. We shouldn't remember, that was the natural order. David understood the significance of the dream as well, it was a kind of memory, an exception to the norm and caused only by the sheer intensity of the trauma. Somehow the memory escaped the confines of the mortal self, had overflowed and burnt itself into the genetic map that would be carried forward into another life. If it is possible for a memory to survive the sterilisation of our spirit during reincarnation, then that memory must have had a monumental impact on us, must have burned so deeply on our soul that its scar could not have been healed. What could be more traumatic than having your leg amputated in that way with no anaesthetic? So, like most of us do, David had allowed his own feelings and experiences to affect his judgement. Perhaps without this mix of the scientist and the man, this investigation would never have begun.

Almost unconsciously he had allowed his ideas to develop.Now he was trying to prove that something finite survived death and even left the body and travelled on elsewhere, perhaps even to a new physical host.

"Four minutes fifty seconds...fifty one...."

David searched the room for any sign of a spirit in transit.

"Monitoring all areas outside the body. No activity at present detectable in proximity to subject. Energy nil. Electrical emissions nil. Magnetic fluctuations nil."

"Come on!"

"Five minutes and eight seconds. Slight magnetic variations directly above patient's head."

David glanced briefly at the others in the room. Saw disbelief on the faces of the medical team. He allowed himself a small laugh, a release.

"Illuminate !".

The air was filled with tiny particles of light emitting material that if biassed correctly would glow when they detected any additional electrical or magnetic emissions. A small negative charge was applied to the atmosphere to raise the bias and the entire room glowed. Then it was reduced fractionally to just below the level at which the light emission was activated.

Time seemed to stand still. Not a breath was taken as they stared intently at the space above the body.

"Five minutes forty seconds. Magnetic field increasing very slightly, now reading at...."

There was a slight crackle like the static on an old fashioned radio. A faint blue haze appeared above the dead man's head.

"Christ!" Michael shouted as he rubbed his eyes and stared at the light. The faint blue cloud now shone brightly assuming an almost ghostly aura and while increasing in intensity it also grew in size as if filling itself from some invisible source below.

Then slowly it began to lift. It drew away leaving a tail that attached itself to the centre of the forehead. As it moved it stretched the spiritual umbilical finger thin and the blue light grew brighter and twinkled with specks of red and silver.

David stared intently, oblivious to the others in the room. Unconsciously he ran his hand across his forehead wiping away the sweat that stung his eyes and trickled down his cheeks. He blinked nervously, frightened in case he should miss anything. The only sounds to be heard above the background drone of machinery and air conditioning was a faint crackle from the spirit.

David felt Michael's hand on his arm, fingers squeez-ing, nails digging in. He gave a nervous, almost self- deprecating laugh that seemed like a roar in his own ears.

Then the mist detached itself from the corpse with what David imagined was an audible "plop". It floated serenely up and across the room as if pulled by an invisible hand. Its shape fluctuated rhythmically, travelling slowly and almost with a motion akin to swimming.

It reached the ceiling and stopped, successfully trapped by the lead alloy lining.

Breaking through the spell that held him frozen for a moment, David focused his mind on the technical aspect of trying to trap the spirit for further examination.

"Try vacuum", he shouted in a nervous, high pitched voice. Michael reached up with a thin pipe towards the mist and the whine of a pump was just audible.

Nothing happened.

"Increase vacuum!"

The pump accelerated, its whine more significant.

The illuminated spirit embedded itself in the corner of the room then slid gently across the ceiling towards the other corner. It flattened itself and hugged the barrier through which it seemed unable to pass. Then it slowly traversed the room as if searching for a way out.

"Electromagnet!" Shouted David.

Michael dropped the vacuum tube and picked up an instrument that looked like a small metal detector which he held up towards the spirit. A faint hum could be heard and the air around the implement's tip began to glow.

At first nothing happened. Then as the saucer shaped tip of the probe almost made contact with the mist the edges appeared to be sucked towards it. The effect was not enough to pull the spirit off course but it seemed to ruffle the edge that was closest to it.

"Increase magnetic field!" David yelled.

The humming of the coils grew louder. The lights in

the room appeared to flicker and the movement of the spirit across the ceiling slowed perceptibly allowing its lower edge to touch the magnetic dish.

"More power!"

The electrical hum increased but was suddenly lost behind the sharp crackle of sound as the haze danced across the probe.

Particles of light emitting dust exploded.

The spirit seemed to stop.

Michael was aware that his hands were shaking and that his mouth felt dry. He gulped nervously but his eyes never left the spirit as he cautiously moved the probe. The spirit moved with it, attached.

The lights definitely dimmed again as the electrical load from the magnetic generator approached the limit available on the hospital circuit.

David quietly cursed himself for having failed to arrange for more power to be available but really it was a contingency he could hardly have envisaged. In truth this was all guess work, virgin territory.

Michael moved towards the alloy container in which they hoped to trap the spirit.

The indicators on the monitors flickered and flashed. Sounds seemed to come from everything around him. Briefly he glanced over at David but quickly, and just in time, he turned back to focus on his progress.

Suddenly there was a flash of brilliant blue light as if every ionised particle in the room had overloaded. He staggered back, losing his balance and letting go of the probe with one hand to steady himself. Blinded and confused he became disorientated and fell, grabbing the computer terminal for support and bringing it crashing to the floor with him. He struck his head against the rack of test equipment as he fell. In the confusion he was sure he saw the door open and the spirit escape.

His last thought before an instant's loss of consciousness was that they had seen it. The experiment was a success and they had nearly trapped what could only have been a human spirit if someone had not ignored the security notice on the door and opened it at the critical time.

Then a moments blackness descended.

Almost immediately Michael's head cleared. He looked anxiously across the room in case he had missed anything. The whole scene seemed strangely back to normal, no unexpected sounds, no sudden flashes of light, nothing out of the ordinary. Nurses were busy clearing up the ward and he recognised the shape of the man on the gurney, now somehow very dead and empty.

He lifted himself on one elbow and dabbed at his forehead where he felt blood trickling down from where he had struck the metal rack.

David and the young intern were coming towards him. The doctor placed a wad of gauze on the small wound and taped it into place.

"Nothing serious, just a scratch."

But Michael was oblivious. His eyes were locked with Davids and he could see the look of triumph in the other man's eyes. He staggered to his feet and put an arm around David's shoulder, hugging him. Suddenly he felt euphoric. The results had been a lot better than they had expected.

"Did you see it David. Did you see the "spirit"!

"Yes Michael, I saw it."

STILLBORN

CHAPTER TWO

It was nearly six months later that David returned to the hospital where they had carried out that first experiment. The research had gone well and both he and the drug company were pleased with the progress that had been made with the Reincarnation research, particularly with the development of a drug that would allow full memory transfer.

The doctor sitting opposite David wasn't one of those who had been present but was a consultant from the medical team.

"I am very sorry, I wish I could have given you better news, but the tests...well...".

The doctor hadn't looked at David until then but had kept his eyes fixed on the papers in his hands which he shuffled through nervously as he spoke. As if compelled, he raised his head and looked at him as he continued.

"There's little point in holding back the truth. You would soon work it out for yourself."

David felt detached, isolated, cut-off. The words seemed so meaningless as if they were discussing someone else. He looked across at the doctor and noticed how he seemed so uncomfortable in his chair, how he looked down at his hands nervously while he spoke and shuffled the pieces of paper that he held.

'I suppose it must be difficult telling somebody that they are dying,' he thought.

Strangely, David felt that he wanted to laugh.

"......it's terminal."

It was as if someone had slammed a door in his face. It was not so much the pronouncement of his impending death but the suddenness of its arrival that shook him.

It was like hearing of the death of a relative who has been ill for some time. It is not the fact itself, watered down as it would be by the knowledge of its imminence, but the cold reality that one had to face. Life is finite but it's end is an unknown, its predictability is illusory. At twenty years of age it is hardly given any thought and even at seventy we can push this unknown barrier away with a hypothetical cushion of a decade or more. It is only when it becomes quantifiable, when you are told it is within weeks or months that it's sting can really be felt.

David had known for sometime that there was something wrong. He probably even had a good idea what it was for he had considerable knowledge of human physiology. Cancer had also been prevalent in his family on his mother's side. Combine these two facts and it was certain that he had repressed the knowledge of his own condition, tucked it away to fester in some recess of his mind. There were other things that were too important, had a greater demand on his time, his work, Judy.

'It's strange how doctors and nurses are the world's worst patients,' he thought. Even he, with his understanding of the disease, had ignored the very obvious symptoms and left things too late.

"Isn't there any chance at all? What about surgery, chemotherapy?" David asked in a weak voice.

"Very little........ I am going to recommend an immediate course of therapy, there may be some remission," this part was easier for the doctor, the human part was the bit he hated. Now he could switch back and hide behind his professional facade, recite medical facts etched in his memory from years of training.

"With secondaries already in your liver and spine..... The best we can expect is nine months to a year. Quality is what counts now, do those things you have been putting off, spoil yourself a bit. The drugs will make sure there isn't too much pain."

"But surely the liver is operable and..." David still desperately sought an avenue of escape.

"Not in your case David. Its just too much and too late. The secondaries are so widespread that the chances of eradicating all cancerous cells is minimal.....You know yourself that once there are secondaries... well....its only a matter of time."

The doctor shrugged apologetically and lowered his eyes. David let his mind wander, not really listening to the doctor's words, his advice, his attempts at painting a not altogether bleak future for David.

'Of course he had known all along,' he told himself. 'After all, most of his family had died at a comparatively early age from cancer in one form or another. His mother had only been fifty-five.'

'Incredible,' he thought. 'With the huge medical advances made during the twentieth century, the cause and cure of cancer still remained a mystery and had even become a greater threat to man as his life expectancy had grown.

Most of the old diseases had been entirely eradicated. Medicine and surgery had evolved incredibly, research into the causes and treatment of disease was on a roller coaster high. Genetic research had reached state of the art. Infant mortality was extremely rare and babies born as prematurely as twenty four weeks and weighing little over a pound were now expected to survive while only twenty years earlier they would have had little chance even at twice the size.

But cancer had eluded every effort made to discover a way to control it. Certainly, if detected early enough and treatment successfully eradicated all cancerous cells, then your prognosis was fair. But that was a treatment, not a preventative measure and even then the disease had a nasty habit of returning. If it managed to spread to the essential organs such as the liver or brain then....'

Coming out of his reverie he saw the doctor was standing, offering him his hand.

'The verdict is over,' he mused. 'Guilty on all charges. Sentenced to death!'

"Yes thank you doctor. I'll think about your recommendations."

"Yes. Please do. Don't forget to book your next appointment with the nurse."

"Oh....yes. How long did you say?"

"A week will be about right."

"What? I thought you said....a year..."

"No, your appointment professor. Come and see me again next week, we can decide on your course of therapy then."

"Oh yes. Sorry. Next week."

David left the building and made his way back across London to his office in Docklands in a daze. As he sat on the underground he noticed an old couple opposite, laughing and joking. Silently he cursed the unknown adjudicator who metered out the lifetimes we should have. It seemed so unfair.

Then he was back in his office trying to work, pushing aside his personal problems and trying to deal with the back log created by his absence that day.

STILLBORN

It didn't work. Each time he tried to focus on the printed words that were on the report he was dealing with, the words would become jumbled and his concentration would slowly give way to that one subject that was predominant in his mind. His death.

He slammed a bony hand on his desk, papers scattered and dropped to the floor. He pulled off his glasses and wiped his eyes with his sleeve.

As he rubbed his tired eyes a vision of Judy flashed before him.

"Oh Christ... Judy", he mumbled disconsolately. He leant forward and buried his face in his hands as he pictured her in his mind.

They had just become engaged and intended getting married later in the year. She was so beautiful, so young. Tall, long hair flowing over suntanned shoulders. Big brown eyes that he felt he would drown in. Just a few months more and they would have been together, her lovely body close to his at night, making love...

Now it would never happen. They had waited so long it seemed and he had been happy with that, it was something to look forward to, to nurture. Although not a Catholic himself he had respected her beliefs and knew instinctively that making love with her would be warm and pleasurable, not like before.

His first marriage had been cold, born out of intellectual compatability instead of emotion. There had been little real love and sex had been perfunctory at best. David knew it wasn't all his wife's fault, that perhaps she had been second in line to his work. It was a common view among his colleagues and friends that he was a bit cold, somewhat insular and detached and definitely too preoccupied with whatever project he was involved with at the time.

His marriage hadn't been all bad either, just too low key. It had just never really blossomed and in truth the little that had bound them together had just slowly evaporated. It was almost as if it had never happened, that marriage.

Twelve years with little to remember.

Then Judy had come into his life and everything had changed. At thirty eight he had felt his first real moment of passion and it had been born in a simple exchange, a meeting of eyes.

David stood up and walked over to the window. He placed his hands on the sill and leant forward so that his forehead touched the cool glass. Raindrops pattered on the other side and ran down the pane, millimetres from his cheek, like tears he had forgotten how to cry.

Cursing inwardly he stood up. Even erect his shoulders slumped and his long hair hung untidily over the collar of his white coat.

He turned away and walked back to his desk. David picked up another report on which he tried to focus but each time he tried to take in the data the words would become blurred and his mind would superimpose those from his medical report: 'Prognosis - poor. Life expectancy - nine to twelve months'. He slammed down the document angrily. In exasperation he strode out of his office, habitually brushing his long hair from his forehead. The door swung to a close behind him, the noise it made the only disturbance in an otherwise empty building.

He made his way down to the ground floor in the lift and walked past the security man at his desk.

STILLBORN

"Good night professor, bit wet," he said cheerfully. David stopped and stared at the man without speaking. He looked at the cherubic red face with its kind eyes and jovial smile without recognition.

Turning, he started towards the door to the street. Only as he pushed against the shining brass plate and stepped out into the rain did he give a reluctant reply.

"Good night."

The security man caught only a mumble but called after the retreating figure in his still cheerful voice.

"See you tomorrow sir. Have a good evening."

It was seven thirty, already dark and quite chilly on this October evening. Most people had left the city much earlier and were already home with their families. David walked slowly along the pavement towards the entrance to the underground, his head bent to shield his eyes from the rain. Someone waved to him as he passed them, a cleaner on their way to work at the CDG laboratories. Lost in thought and self pity, he either didn't see them, or determinedly avoided their gaze. He passed the flower shop and newsagents, now closed and dimly lit. Suddenly he stopped and looked around as if uncertain as to where he was. He looked towards the station entrance and slowly back along the street to where he stood, glancing at the closed shop fronts but without really taking them in. Then his eyes stopped at the little pub just three doors away.

'Funny,' he mumbled to himself. 'I've been working here for six months and I never noticed it before.'

As he walked on a couple came out of the door laughing and David glanced inside. Only a few drinkers remained, perched on bar stools, glasses in their hands. It was one of those city pubs, packed at lunch times and for an hour or so after work when people stopped off for a drink on the way home.

David didn't socialise much and drank even less, just a sherry before Sunday lunch or a glass of wine when having dinner with colleagues or relatives. He couldn't remember ever going into a pub on his own although he supposed he had done when he was younger.

On impulse he grabbed at the closing door and stepped into the brightly lit bar. As it swung closed behind him he stood for a moment and shook the rain from his jacket and wiped the wet hair from his forehead. Uncertainly he walked up to the deserted end of the bar and sat on a bar stool.

The barman came up to him and nodded.

"What's your poison?" He asked in a thick East-end accent.

"What?" David asked, his mind still absorbed with his own thoughts and not really taking in the man's words.

"What do you want to drink guv?" The barman had a smile on his face. "This is a pub you know."

"Oh yes.....drink. I'll......" he gazed around at the bottles looking for something familiar then quickly took in the others in the bar, two young men in business suits talking animatedly, small glasses in their hands. Another group of six, men and women who looked like shop workers, their dress less formal. The women with glasses of wine, the men with pints of beer.

"Well?"

"Yes..a drink. I'll have a...a beer."

"Lager, bitter, wot's it to be guv? You look like you

need something to pick you up. Try an export gold, that should do the trick."

Yes...yes an export...a pint I think."

"Coming right up guv!" The barman leant over and picked up a glass and waved it at David.

"Straight glass alright or want a handle?"

"No that's fine, thank you."

"Work 'round ere?"

"Yes..at the moment. CDG, just down the road."

"Oh you're a boffin then. Scientist I s'pose."

"Research. I'm involved in research."

The barman placed the now full glass in front of David.

"There you go then prof, do a bit of research on that then! One pound eighty."

David put his hand in his pocket and pulled out some change. He handed over the correct amount of money.

"Thanks prof"

He walked down the bar and put the money in the till before turning to one of the men in the group of six.

"Hey Burt, we got ourselves a professor from that CDG place. Funny sort of geezer, seems like 'ees in a world of 'is own if you ask me."

David was vaguely aware of the whispered conversation but was already too involved in his own thoughts to take any notice or realise that the other man had turned to look at him. He picked up the glass and sipped, hardly tasting the strong lager as it went down. His mind was already deeply involved in its own machinations, the liquid that entered his mouth now smelt of medicine but that was only because his subconscious wanted it to.

'Cancer medicine,' he thought glumly.

He took another mouthful and it now reminded him

30

of a bygone age, syrup of figs or castor oil. He nursed the drink in his hand and stared forward gloomily for sometime until almost inevitably his thoughts turned back to Judy. The next time he lifted the glass to his lips he was certain the aroma was that of her body and her perfume and when he sipped it there was the taste of her lips mingled with that slightly salty taste of her tears...........

A few miles away Michael Tamasoto relaxed in his apartment, his wife Hannah having gone to her weekly art class at the local Adult Education Centre.
He enjoyed these times when he could be on his own and reflect. Although he was a very physical man, he was also fairly analytical, even introspective.
'It was strange,' he thought. 'How people classified you because of your appearance or how they perceived you to be.' He supposed he was quite unusual having so many opposing facets to his personality. Most people were either one thing or another, academic or physical, strong or emotional. Michael was aware that he had many aspects to his nature that most would consider incongruous. He seemed to have been blessed with equally high levels of physical and mental ability and was at the same time an emotional man but one with plenty of self-confidence.
Michael lay back on the couch and began to consider the day's events. Beside him on a low table was a drink from which he occasionally took a sip. In the background classical music flowed gently through the room.
Michael was worried about David. His friend had been acting strangely the last few days, he seemed even more preoccupied than usual. He didn't look well

either, his face was drawn and had a slightly grey tinge to it.

As he thought about David the relaxed smile on his face faded. He had known there was something wrong recently but had just put it down to over-work. At the best of times David's intensity about his work bordered on obsession and it had always been difficult to get him to unwind and enjoy himself. Michael was probably one of the few friends who could manage this and when they were out together it usually didn't take that long before he could distract David with a few jokes and put a smile on his face.

Michael had nothing but respect for David. He had known him for five years now ever since he first came to London. Apart from their shared interests in the research projects they had also become firm friends and often spent an evening together, with Judy and Hannah. It was an unusual friendship, both men having very different qualities and interests and the friendship would probably have never occurred if they hadn't been thrown together by their work. Strangely it was a friendship that worked, a case of opposites attracting, and they were certainly very different. Michael's upbringing couldn't have been more unlike David's and while his friend was a pure academic, Michael was more of a physical being who had ended up working with David more by chance than through choice.

He had spent most of his earlier years in San Francisco living with his grandparents. His grandfather was Japanese and had migrated there at the turn of the century, marrying an American woman of Mexican extraction.

Michael's mother had died when he was still young

while giving birth to his sister, Rebecca. His father had never really recovered from the loss and had compensated by throwing himself into his profession as a mining engineer, work which would take him anywhere in the world at a moment's notice. From then on Michael and Rebecca had lived with their grandparents most of the time and the biggest influence during Michael's formative years had been his grandfather.

His appearance belied his mixed race parentage, one quarter Japanese and one quarter Mexican. The remaining fifty percent had provided him with his Anglo Saxon appearance; tall, broad shouldered and with blue eyes.

The only tell tale signs were in the well tanned skin, the lank black hair. Perhaps something in the eyes, a slight up-turn of the corners and an ability to hide his emotions. Inside there was a lot of Japanese, not all of it planted genetically, much of it as a result of his Grandfather's influence. Michael had loved his grandfather and they had spent much time together when he was a child with Michael listening to the old man's stories of his family and times in Tokyo before the first World War. Later as a teenager in San Francisco, Michael could be found mixing more with the young Japanese population, he joined a club, trained in martial arts as a hobby, tried to become as Japanese as he could to please his grandfather.

At college he had excelled in all sports, particularly American football in which he had rapidly become a rising star. Alongside his academic work he spent a lot of his time training and competing and even as a freshman it seemed that his career would be on the field instead of in the laboratory.

STILLBORN

That was until he was injured and his football career came to an unexpected end. The accident had occurred during a particularly hard fought game. His team were trailing, the opposition were tough. Their forwards were big and tackled ruthlessly. Michael, as receiver, took a long pass but as he caught the ball he was swamped by the chasing pack intent on killing the play quickly. He fell awkwardly, three huge forwards landing on top of him. It was a freak accident and Michael was left with a badly fractured pelvis and a ruptured spleen which almost cost him his life.

The after effect was double edged. While his football career came to an abrupt end he immediately compensated by putting all his efforts into his studies, eventually leaving college with distinctions. He had then worked for several US drug companies, his skills in biochemistry and particularly as an analyst ensured that there were many opportunities for him to advance his career.

Michael had chosen to stay close to home, still bound to his beloved grandfather who had given him so much during his childhood and who had become old and frail with the passing of the years. It wasn't until the old man's death that Michael had decided to make a change and had taken the job with CDG in London.

All of this had combined to make Michael unique. He had acquired a very different outlook on life to his workmates and friends, particularly here in Europe. This caused him to live a fairly withdrawn, insular life. It wasn't that he had difficulty in making friends but that the difference in his outlook gave him little in common with people he met through his work. He certainly couldn't imagine David enjoying the fresh air and open spaces and most of

the people he came into contact with were the same.
Intense and introvert, less physical than he.

Most, not all though. Judy was perhaps an exception
having many similarities to the people that he had
grown up with. It was her vitality that made her stand
out. Physically she was exceptional as well, with long
legs and a slim but strong body, silken hair and sparkling eyes. He smiled to himself as he pictured her.
She was beautiful, David was so lucky and didn't even
know it.

'It was strange,' he mused. 'How a man like himself
had somehow married one of the introvert types so
typical of the academic world in which he lived and
with whom he really had little in common. David on
the other hand, the archetype academic, was to marry
the beautiful and very physical Judy.

As he considered his lot he sighed and took a large
mouthful of the drink, perhaps attempting to subdue
the feeling of disquiet this train of thought provoked.
Oh he loved Hannah, he assured himself. Perhaps not
quite with the same intensity as at first but he did
care for her even though they seemed to have so little
in common and found little to talk about these days,
except their work.

His mind wandered, consciously avoiding the subject
of Hannah and returning to Judy and David and his
own childhood. He reached back into the archives of
his memory and pictured the first time that he had
stepped out onto the football field for a major league
game. For a moment he experienced the giddiness he
had felt as he left the tunnel to emerge before
thousands of cheering fans. He could taste the
adrenaline, smell the fear.

He stood up and walked around the room lost in

memories of his home and childhood. He looked out of the window and saw the very different people of London, scurrying about, wrapped up in warm clothes, jackets, long coats - heads bent down to avoid the cold drizzle.

As he watched his memories faded, the reality of the present breaking through into his consciousness. It brought back his worries about David.

He turned away from the window, allowing his past to overlap the present once again as he remembered the time that they had met, when he had been assigned to work as David's assistant.

Of course Michael had been fully aware of David's reputation and he had felt particularly honoured at his appointment. But it was with pleasure and surprise that he had discovered a special rapport existed between them. It was not very long before they became close personal friends as well. The fact that Michael, at thirty three, was quite a bit younger than David didn't make much difference either. In some ways he was a lot more mature than David who had spent his life in universities and research laboratories and knew little of the real world. Michael admired David's single mindedness, perhaps that ability to focus on their work was something that they shared. He was not overwhelmed by him though, perhaps a little envious of the respect that David received but he appeared not to even be aware of it. If that jealousy did exist, it was well hidden and probably had little to do with their work but more to do with their women.

Michael took another drink, tried to shrug off the disquieting thoughts that kept returning of their own accord. He was the kind of man who kept his private feelings to himself, buried deep inside where neither he nor others could see them. Sometimes though, when the four of them were together, his eyes would wander appraisingly from Hannah to Judy.

He was sure that neither woman was aware of his controlled interest in Judy and even Michael himself had not recognised the faint mental murmurings behind his sparkling eyes as he subconsciously compared them.

Michael lifted his head and shook back his dark hair. His blue eyes sparkled as he pictured his friend sitting at his computer terminal absorbed in his work, living in his own private little world.

The following morning David arrived at the laboratory later than usual. Michael was already busy studying some slides under the microscope but looked up when David entered the room.

"Hi David, how are things?....Jonas wants to see you."

"Thanks Michael," David's voice was edgy. "Don't know what he wants, do you? I'm behind as it is."

"He just said for you to go straight up to his office. Seemed quite cheerful though."

David opened his briefcase and pulled out some papers which he quickly shuffled through. Without looking up at Michael he turned to leave but Michael didn't want to let the conversation go. They had hardly talked recently and he was still worried about David who looked even more drawn and intense than usual.

STILLBORN

"How's the lovely Judy?"

He sighed and dropped the papers he was holding on to his desk.

"She's fine."

"When are you two going to name the day? I thought it was full steam ahead now".

"I don't know. It isn't that simple right now, especially as we are getting near to the end of the reincarn program".

"Near the end. What are you talking about?" He looked at David more carefully, noticing the preoccupied expression. "It could be years before we get approval from the B.M.A and that's only the beginning. Then we'll need to carry out all those clinical tests on humans before the results can be released. It could take forever before we are finished with the project. You could be an old man by then."

Michael looked at him with amusement in his eyes. It was so typical of David to be vague about his personal life. His work came before just about everything. Even Judy, he mused.

"Come on, I didn't mean it that literally. I'd just like to have the tests over and done with so that I can have a clear desk and take a bit of time off."

David hoped the conversation would end there but Michael was obviously not going to let it go.

"Well, why don't you both come over tonight. The girls would like to see each other again and we could talk about it then?"

"Sorry I can't. Not tonight. Anyway I must get up to see Jonas. Don't want to upset the boss."

He smiled and got up to leave but Michael put out a hand and caught his shoulder as he was about to turn away. There was obvious concern on his face.

"Come over on Thursday then. Help celebrate
Hannah's birthday," he said with quiet insistence. "We
can all go out for a meal, you've got to take a break
sometime or other. If not you might as well move in
here and take up residence," then with a broad smile,
he added. "With a girl like Judy ready and waiting,
you really do get your priorities wrong sometimes.
Come on!"

"Oh...oh all right. I'll have a word with Judy, she's
bound to agree with you. But we can't stay too long,
I don't want another of your all night sessions."

"Ok. Thursday. And no excuses!"

"Look," he glanced at the clock distractedly, "I must
get up to Jonas, I'll see you later."

David took the opportunity to leave quickly before
his friend could object but not without Michael
noticing how agitated he was.

Michael paused in thought as he watched him disappear around a corner and wondered why David had
been acting so strangely lately.

David, on the other hand, didn't even consider that
he was behaving in an unusual way. Being so wrapped
up in his own gloomy thoughts, together with his
normal preoccupation with his work, he didn't give
his chat with Michael another thought as he made his
way quickly to Jonas's office. So far he had avoided
telling anyone about his problem but he knew he
would have to, sooner or later.

Later rather than sooner, he decided.

As he stood in the lift he couldn't help worrying why
Jonas had called him in and whether someone had
told him? Shit! He thought, they couldn't take him
off the program.

He carried on down the corridor lost in thought until

he found himself outside Jonas's door. He stopped and hitched up his trousers, noticing that he was still losing weight. It was not that he had ever been really big but now when he looked at himself in the mirror in the mornings he seemed even more gaunt by the day.

'Still,' he reassured himself. 'At least I have my work.'

He ran his fingers nervously through his hair and straightened himself up before pushing the door open and stepping into the reception area. Jonas's secretary looked up at him with a professional smile on her lips and was just about to speak.

"Come right in David," a rich voice called from the inner sanctum, somehow aware of David's presence.

"Go right head professor," the secretary added.

He made his way through the reception area where Jonas loved to keep members of his staff waiting and into his office.

Jonas Nichols, the departmental manager, was a big man even by today's standards. At six foot six and weighing over one hundred and twenty kilograms, his size belied his intelligence. Droopy eyelids hid sparkling blue eyes, the impassive face disguised a lively intellect and boundless energy when it came to his first love, work, and in particular how his efforts could provide him with promotion and more power.

"Sit down David," The big man boomed at him. "Want a drink?"

"Coffee will be fine," he replied as he followed Jonas's waving finger to a chair where he deposited himself limply. Almost as soon as David was seated, the secretary brought the coffee and put it on the table. Jonas demonstrated his present affability by pouring it. Then he leant forward and asked in an unusually mild tone of voice.

"Now David. How close are we really on the reincarn program? I've read your reports, they really are amazing," his eyes focused on David for a second before he swung around and gazed out of the window. "But I have to keep the directors up to date. You understand, to keep the funds rolling in."

After a few moment's silence, while Jonas seemed to be concentrating on something far away, he suddenly turned back and continued. "I know you and your assistant have been working very hard."

David noticed how he didn't refer to Michael by name but then he knew of Jonas's dislike for foreigners and because of Michael's mixed race ancestry and the fact that he was an American, he would classify him as such.

"Very close Jonas. I'm certain the latest drug test on the monkeys has proved all our theories. Cellar 2, is fourteen weeks old now and we tried one of the memory tests yesterday. It scored immediately!"

"Yes. Yes. I read the report. But what about a human test? When can that be attempted?"

"The problem there is with the B.M.A. Until we have been through all the usual procedures we can't test on a human. Even if we doubled up on staff and resources, it could take three or four years. I know the budget won't run to that."

"But the tests will be carried out on the dead. Surely the same rules don't apply?"

"No. The injection of the drug has to be given before death. I know it's only just a minute or two but you know what the B.M.A are like."

"Couldn't we stretch the rules a bit? I mean if it's

only moments before death, who is to know?"

David looked more carefully at Jonas. 'What is he getting at?' He asked himself.

"Possibly. We might get around that one with the permission of the family. What about the recipient, the foetus and the mother?"

"We won't be trying any drugs out on them, will we?"

"No. I suppose not......It's just the whole process, there are too many risks. I don't know if we'd get away with it."

'God! What am I saying?' David asked himself. 'What is happening to my ethics? What does Jonas expect of me?'

"No Jonas. I just couldn't go along with it - we will have to wait."

"I see," Jonas seemed to squint. "How long was it that you said. Three or four years?"

'Damn!' Thought Jonas. 'I can't wait that long!'

'Damn!' Thought David. 'I'll be dead before then!'

There was a pause as each considered this problem. When Jonas did eventually break the silence his words were like a bombshell to David.

"David.... I know about your problem. We haven't got three or four years."

"But..How...?"

"Let's just say I have my sources. Don't worry about that now, it's just as important for me to see this program through as quickly as possible and you are the man to do it," then, almost as an afterthought, he added. "Look...I'm er, very sorry."

Jonas's eyes sparkled even as he spoke these words of commiseration. David felt shocked at the apparent humour in the big man's eyes and then began to wonder why it was there. Jonas hadn't just called him in to be sympathetic, there was more going on in this man's head than pity.

David said nothing but looked down at his hands, wondering what was coming next.

"I have an idea."

For a split second David felt a lift, a splattering of hope. Then, he logically concluded, perhaps Jonas's real concern was the reincarn program, not David. His shoulders sagged and he felt his moment of hope evaporate.

"David. What if there was a candidate? Someone who took it upon themselves to break a few rules and try the drug.... come to some private arrangement with the recipient."

"What would be the point. Unless they were prepared to die as well, the drug...."

David broke off suddenly and looked back into those twinkling eyes. 'Christ!' He wondered. 'Was Jonas suggesting what he thought? Surely not that he should try the drug himself'.

David didn't react immediately but considered this new suggestion before jumping to conclusions. 'It was crazy', he thought. 'But then again, why not!' He could set up the whole thing without involving anyone else. He was dying anyway, what had he to lose by becoming a guinea pig himself. When they were ready all he had to do was to take the drug, then, his own life. He could really see if he was right then, if he could survive death and reincarnation and remember it all. What an opportunity!

"Yes. Yes it's possible. Think of the time that would be saved," David couldn't contain the feelings that were welling up inside him. Elation and hope showed in his eyes and speech. "It'll need a lot of working

out. A lot of preparation. But....but, yes it's
possible. I probably have a year, maybe longer with
the right medication. I could do it..."
"Of course I don't know what you are suggesting,"
interrupted Jonas with a beaming smile and a wink.
"The records will show that this was just a routine
meeting. No tapes, nothing on file," he leant forward
and adopted a more serious expression. "But think
David! If you were successful, your achievement
would be very prestigious....and as a bonus you will
survive this illness that will otherwise end your life.
Perhaps even work something out with Judy if you
wanted to. Despite the er, age difference." Jonas's
smile turned into a laugh. David forgot his problems
for a moment and caught up by Jonas's enthusiasm
found himself laughing as well.

Jonas Nichols was a shrewd and calculating man. He
had watched David's face intently as he had talked,
especially noting the sparkle of eagerness as he had
held out the carrot, the chance that this would give
David of living and perhaps even fulfilling his
relationship with Judy. It was at that moment that he
knew David would do as he wished and while his
subordinate rambled on about his work, Jonas let his
thoughts drift towards his own ambitions and the
prestige and the power that such a success in his
department would bring. While smiling across at
David, he was really seeing images of his own
future. Perhaps a seat on the Board.
'And then what?' He asked himself. 'A few more years
and old John Chandler would have to step down as
Chairman and let a younger man take over. Someone
like himself with his knowledge and strength would

surely be noticed. You only had to look at the other old men on the Board, just filling in the days until they too retired, to know he stood a good chance.'

Like all leaders and entrepreneurs, Jonas was certain that destiny held great things for him. In the same way as he was doing now, he often indulged himself in mental scenarios where he, Jonas Nichols, was awarded the highest of accolades. The day dream collapsed when his reverie was disturbed by David getting to his feet. He focused on the untidy little man before him and forced the sneer on his face back into a smile.

"Well... I'd better get back to work. The preparations will take time and time is something I am running out of."

"Yes, you do that."

As David rose to leave Jonas glanced up at him again.

"Don't forget to keep comprehensive evidence. Plenty of taped notes and video. After all you may not be in a position to report directly to me for some time!"

Jonas's laughter echoed behind him as he left but David was lost in his own thoughts and was already planning ahead. Then in the middle of his euphoria an image of Judy implanted itself in his mind and his mood became suddenly more pensive.

'What can I tell Judy?'

STILLBORN

CHAPTER THREE

Judy wasn't as fragile as David would like to think. It wasn't that she was insensitive or that she had about her any lack of femininity but like most young women of the twentieth century she was quite self sufficient and filled her equal role in society with confidence and certainly, with just as much effectiveness as her male counterparts.

Of course, women always have provided a certain strength that is not often found in men and in these more evolved times, they were able to express themselves more fully than their predecessors had been given the opportunity to do.

At twenty three, Judy was an attractive and intelligent young woman. Trained in biochemistry, she worked as a senior laboratory technician for CDG where she and David had met. She lived in a small, modern apartment in London's dock-side development, a legacy from her parents.

Before meeting David she had not found the need to commit herself to anyone although she had enjoyed many boyfriends but for some reason none of her relationships had developed into anything worthwhile or lasting.

Unusually for these times she was 'almost' a virgin. Not quite, because at eighteen, while her parents had been away on holiday she had drunk too much and slept with a man. It had not been good, he had used her and left and she had felt a little self-disgust which only helped her adhere to her Catholic upbringing. It was also strange because Judy had mixed feelings about many of the edicts of her church and was not afraid to question them. At the same time she was sexually aware, had strong feelings and was easily aroused.

Her upbringing had left its mark. The convent schools, her own religious beliefs and above all the love and trust that her parents had shown her and the example those two good people had set and which she tried her best to follow. It is possible that to some extent she hid behind the church's rulings, not really believing in them but using them as a mask. On one hand her first experience with a man had been bad and almost at the same time she suffered the sudden death of her parents which had also hurt her badly. In contrast she was well aware of the strength of her desires about which she had been brought up to feel guilt but which on a personal level she accepted as both natural and healthy. It was an enigma, she was at a cross roads, like a little explosion which was ready to happen. If she stepped in one direction, she could do so with a vengeance and quickly forget the other. Then she had met David during a seminar at London University where he was the guest speaker. It was a relationship that she slid into easily, she felt secure. He was older than her, could smooth out all the ups and downs of living while she could control him, set the pace of their relationship.

The first time she had actually seen him was as he stood at the lectern giving his oration and she was impressed with the energy and enthusiasm that exuded from his eyes, the rich tones of his voice and more than anything, the vast extent of his knowledge in his chosen field. David Hawkin had a widespread reputation for his achievements and was revered throughout the scientific community for the advances he had made in explaining the link between the physical processes of the brain and the psychic powers of the mind.

Their courtship did not really begin until sometime later when they met again at CDG, David having taken up residence there to carry out his research that CDG were funding.

Their relationship began slowly, borne out of an interest in each other that to start with had been very casual but which grew in to something more than just shared mutual interests. At first it was just a moment shared in the staff canteen when they would merely sense each other's presence. While sipping her coffee, Judy would become aware of the distant feeling of an intrusion into her consciousness and when turning, she would see him looking at her. Sometimes it happened the other way around when he would become aware of her, but in each case a smile would light his face which she would find difficult not to return. After a while they got to know each other a little more and they would spend time together during breaks discussing their work projects or just chatting about the normal day to day occurrences that had befallen them. Slowly, a bond was formed, not only based on work but through that eternal magic that has brought men and women together since time began.

Sometimes Judy wondered at her feelings for David. For a start he was quite a lot older than her and there were also obvious physical disparities. He was on the slim side and quite short and he was certainly not a very physical man. She glanced at herself in the mirror and turned to appreciate her own appearance. The reflected image showed the power in her body and

while not having a large frame or breasts, her body
spelt health and strength. She was nearly three inches
taller than David at five feet ten and weighed a touch
under 70kgs, but every gram was muscle and positioned accurately to give her the healthy appearance
of a well trained athlete. Her hair hung silkenly to
her thighs when loose although often she kept it coiled
around her head for convenience sake. Her skin shone
with a perfect tan all over and her legs were long and
emanated strength although they were by no means
mannish even though her small pert buttocks were
more what you would have expected from a boy than
a woman in her twenties. She liked her body and enjoyed the sensations that she felt. She had always enjoyed physical things and had been very good at most
sports while at university. Her sexual feelings had
begun early and she had become very aware of the
way her own body responded even before she was
thirteen.

Momentarily she was lost in thought as she delved
into her memory while gazing absently at her own
naked image. But as her preoccupation gave way to
the present, she felt a rush of blood to her cheeks and
that warm feeling beginning between her thighs. Pro-
vocatively, now the game had begun, she lifted her
hands to her breasts. Her finger tips brushed her nipples and she felt an increase in the other sensations
within her body. Abruptly she turned and as if dis-
missing some unwanted interruption, she stepped
quickly into the shower and turned it on. The erotic
spell was broken as the jets of luke warm water
brought goose pimples out on her skin. She shivered
and adjusted the tap until it was comfortable then
picked up the shower gel and lathered her body. As

she washed she hummed to herself and let her mind go blank, relaxing in her cocoon of warm water.

After ten minutes self indulgence in the warmth of the water and her own private thoughts, she stepped out of the cubicle and wrapped herself in the comforting softness of a large fluffy towel before walking to her living room where she lay down on the couch. Almost immediately a faint buzz alerted her and she reached over and picked up the phone.

"Judy, how are you?" David's voice seemed stilted, preoccupied with something.

That wasn't unusual and Judy smiled to herself.

"Hi David, are you still at work? Are you coming over?"

"I'm working late but I should be finished soon...... Judy," he paused and Judy detected a seriousness that made her a little uneasy, "There have been a few developments that I want to tell you about."

"Well..when will I see you?"

"In an hour or so if that's all right?"

"Of course it is. Shall I get some food in or do you want to eat out?"

"No let's stay in so we can talk."

Once again she felt slightly uncomfortable, probably because he was so serious and before he had called she had been feeling so relaxed. She shrugged as if to dismiss the thought. After all David was always a little on the serious side. Still, she thought, something was bothering him.

"You sound worried David. There is something wrong isn't there?" She paused, then with an effort shrugged off the disquieting feeling. "Do you want anything special tonight?"

"No," he said defensively. "I just want to talk to you

Judy, just spend a little time on our own."

"No," she laughed, "I mean is there anything special you'd like to eat?"

David didn't respond with laughter as she might have expected, just gave her a serious reply.

"You choose, I'll be there in about an hour. See you then."

"Ok David.... I love you......", the words hung there unheard. As soon as she started to utter them she heard the click before his voice was replaced by the dialling tone.

Judy sighed. The one thing that sometimes aggravated her about David was his intenseness, particularly when he started to talk about his work. Sometimes she felt so left out, an incidental in his life which seemed so taken up with his research. She sighed, it looked like being another one of those evenings when David spoke excitedly about his research and Judy listened attentively. Not that Judy wasn't fascinated by David's reincarn program but there were other things in life and it was nice sometimes just to snuggle up in the warm and enjoy a bit of music or a video. She sighed again and as if to break her train of thought she sat up abruptly and scrabbled on the table for her directory. Finding the correct number she telephoned and ordered pizzas.

Putting down the phone she picked up the TV control box, switched on and flicked through the channels before stopping on BBC2 where they were showing an old American film set on a Californian beach. She laid her head back on the cushions and while vaguely watching the television she allowed her mind to wander again. It was one of those days, she decided, when you just want to laze around and dream. Lost in thought she gazed abstractedly at one particularly well built young man and her eyes followed the camera as it panned slowly up his body. How unlike David he was, she mused, so obviously masculine. Then lost in her dream she suddenly found herself staring into a smiling sun tanned face and jumped with surprise as she saw it was the face of Michael. Almost immediately the mental image she had created readjusted itself and she felt a hot flush of embarrassment colour her cheeks as she realised, that wrapped up in her sensuous feeling of warmth and well-being, her subconscious had played a little trick on her.

'....but Michael, why him?' She asked herself.

It was some time later, Judy and David had eaten and were sitting on the couch. David had surprised Judy by bringing home a bottle of wine, his interest in alcohol was minimal, to him it was just a social nicety. Since he had known about his illness he had started drinking more than usual but Judy hadn't really noticed anything out of the ordinary. Tonight though, he had drunk more than Judy, which in itself was quite unusual.

Now the bottle was empty and in normal circumstances the couple would have been in a nicely relaxed mood.

These were not normal circumstances. David had needed a drink, it helped with the pain but most importantly he hoped it would help him with what he had to tell Judy. At the best of times he found it difficult to talk to anyone about personal matters and these were definitely not the best of times.

"Judy. There's something I have got to tell you........its something pretty bad."

"Hey David! What's wrong with you?" She looked into his eyes, saw the strain around them, felt her concern for him increase. "You've been working too hard, you take everything so seriously and you look so tired."

Judy looked at him again more carefully this time and her face showed her concern. He did look tired, he had lost weight and there were shadows beneath his eyes which appeared even more sunken than usual. Damn his project, she thought, he was always so involved in his work, always putting in an incredible number of hours and making such an effort that he gave little regard for himself. He probably hadn't been eating properly lately or remembering to take his vitamin supplements either.

"Oh David, come here," she snuggled up closer on the couch and pulled his head to her breast. David stiffened and half turning took both her hands in his. "Judy I'm...I'm ill."

She sensed something. Suddenly she was afraid. Taking his face in her hands she looked searchingly into those mournful eyes.

"Ill? I'm not surprised. You must be run down, you are just tired and that's not surprising considering the hours that you have been putting in lately. I'm always telling you that you should take more time off, spend more time with me. You are so.... so intense, so wrapped up in your work. Have you seen a doctor?"

He grasped her wrists and made her look at him, made her stop talking.

"Its got nothing to do with work Judy," he said gently. "You must have noticed the weight I've lost."

He hesitated for a few seconds, afraid to look straight

into her eyes. For a moment he was back at the hospital listening to the pronouncement of his death, seeing the doctor sombrely shake his head as he spoke those words.

"I'm dying Judy"

For a second they stared at each other then Judy pulled David's head back onto her breast and gently stroked his forehead. She didn't say anything, didn't ask any questions but as soon as his head was buried against her, a tear formed in the corner of her eye and rolled slowly down her cheek. They stayed like that for sometime, David afraid to say anything and Judy not wanting to, giving herself time to absorb those words, "I'm dying", not self pityingly, not only with thought of her impending loss but just taking time to accept the fact and to think how she could make it easier for David and to wonder how she herself would manage without him.

Eventually she unwrapped herself from his arms and stood up. Slowly and without sound she led him gently to the bedroom where she sat with him on the side of the bed. Then she put her hands on his face and softly, very softly, brushed his lips with hers.

"I love you, David."

"I love you too, Judy. I'm so sorry."

"Shh..... don't be sorry for me my love. Let's not talk about it. Not now. Not tonight."

Gently she pressed him back onto the bed and when he began to protest she placed her forefinger against his lips and kissed his cheek before slowly standing. Then her hands went to her hair and as he realised what she was about to do he could feel the excitement rise within him. Despite what he felt, he tried to stop her.

"Judy..."

"No David. Let me."

She could feel the excitement rise within her. This time it was un-stoppable. She was doing what she felt was right. She was in control.

"But we can't. You're a Catholic, you said..."

"Oh David... screw the church. I'll get my penance later. It all seems so silly now," she tossed her head back with a gentle laugh and loosened her hair. She was very beautiful, all the more because now she was filled with her own sexuality. Her eyes became somehow wild, her nostrils were slightly flared and knowing the control that she now had only increased her desire to seduce him.

"Just leave it to me. I know what I am doing."

She stood upright beside the bed and after dimming the lights and putting on some background music he had never heard before, she bent down and took something from a draw. She placed the small crumpled cigarette into her mouth and lit the end of it. David guessed what it was and while mildly shocked was at the same time excited. He'd never experimented with dope, even during his university days.

She breathed in deeply, sucking air and smoke into her lungs as the tip glowed. Then she leant over him and placed it between his lips.

"Draw the smoke in and hold it there a second."

He tried and coughed a little. There was a harsh burning sensation but at the same time an unexpected sweetness. He tried again tentatively and it seemed easier. She lay down next to him and snuggled up close sharing the drug with him. After a while he relaxed. Time seemed to lose its perspective, and her face, close to his, seemed to soften. For no reason at all he could feel himself smile and when he looked at her he noticed her eyes were laughing back at him. He laughed too, he just couldn't stop himself.

"Where d'you get it?" He felt so warm and very sexy. His hand touched her face and he looked into her eyes which were like huge pools. Pools in which he was drowning.

"Oh it's easy, anywhere."

For a second she looked straight into his eyes and then slowly extricated herself from his arms. He watched her in awe, a silly little smile was on his face which soon evaporated as she slowly began to undress. As she did so, she swayed gently to the music. David was so taken with her beauty and the excitement that was mounting uncontrollably within him, that he abandoned any further protest. He felt his own desire increasing, was aware of a faint drumming, his pulse, of the sound of his own breathing. All his worries forgotten, deprived of such emotion for so long, he felt an incredible sense of well being and a tremendous desire to reach up and take Judy in his arms. At the same time he was afraid to move or speak in case he broke the spell that she was weaving. He stared intently into her eyes, his peripheral vision taking in the movements of her hands and body, eagerly seeking a glimpse of her breasts. He noticed the way her full lips were parted invitingly and the widening of her eyes as the small drops of perspiration formed on her forehead. He felt lifted by the animal allure she emanated, her limbs seemed so long, she gave out such strength and he wanted some of it, to share in the ritual.

He was transfixed, unable to move or speak. The time trick caused by the drug was wonderful, these moments seemed to have been going on for ever, would continue forever.

"I want you David," her voice was a gentle hiss like that of a coiled snake ready to strike. He couldn't answer.

Now she stood before him completely naked, her beauty amazing him. She let her hands touch her cheeks and travel slowly down her body as she had done many times on her own. Her head arched back and exposed her pulsing throat, offering it to him, teasing him.

She allowed her hands to caress her breasts in a rhythmic way, in tune with the music. Parting her fingers she let her stiffened nipples slide between them. Her breathing was now quite rapid and her desire was total, a desire that had to be fulfilled by him so that she could be complete in every way. Then, slowly, sensuously, she stepped onto the bed and sat astride him before leaning forward and once more letting her lips brush his. She felt the warmth of his body and his arms slowly, tentatively, enshroud her. She pushed them back to the pillow. His mouth parted, his breath became more audible coming in small eager gulps. Then her tongue darted between his lips, between his open teeth, teasing, stimulating, exploring, the moisture within their mouths meeting, spreading, suffusing. She knew her hair was gently brushing his face, she could feel his eagerness as her breasts touched him.

Then her hands started to undress him. He lay back, eyes closed, as he felt her fingers on his skin and her lips tasting first his face then gently down his neck onto his chest. Her lips teased his and withdrew. He felt her tongue flicker against his throat and on down to his chest. Down, down, until he thought he would explode. He could feel her long hair brushing his thighs and thought he would die from the excruciating sweetness of her, felt her lips caress his body until he wanted to crush her to him but was unable. Then slowly, very slowly she lowered her moist body onto his and as she did so his senses were overwhelmed, music seemed to reach his ears, his sense of touch became indescribably sensitive.

It was the same for her, wonderful and fulfilling. Two mature adults both experiencing beautiful sensations that they shared for the first time, both filled with joy and incredulity and the feeling that their lives had been meaningless before this moment. Their inexperience together didn't matter for Judy had been through this a thousand times in her mind and was in complete control. David was going crazy, all but giving in to the desire to obtain release but his maturity in years, his faith in Judy and the overwhelming desire to prolong this moment sustained him.

They made love, slowly and tenderly. Judy controlling, David eagerly responding. Their love making was deep and sincere, not a moments gratification but a coming together, giving and receiving as love making should be.

It was a long time before they were through even though they were so eager. Their desire to perpetuate this bliss was strong and the drug helped their resolve. Then as her climax approached and he sensed it, so he released his own self control. Their bodies moved faster, in unison, she driving, he responding. His hands searched her, felt the muscle spasms, grasped her, squeezed. His own body was rigid, arching up to go as deep as he could into her.

She screamed.

Then it was over, an explosion, Judy laughing and crying at the same time. Tears streaming down a face full of joy, David afraid in case he had hurt her. In all the years of his marriage he had never seen such joy on his wife's face, it was the first time he had witnessed the pleasure that a woman could feel, when it transcended happiness, seemed like pain.

He asked her if she was alright, his voice deeper than usual, still trembling from the passion.

She laughed, the joy magnified by the tears.

"Oh yes my darling...I'm just happy..it was so good."

Then seeing her tears were of pleasure, he relaxed and felt laughter rise in his chest too.

She felt fulfilled, the dream she had lived a thousand times had become a reality.

He felt a complete man for the first time in his life. Emotionally as well as physically, for the first time.....

And maybe the only time....

His laughter subsided and he felt an overwhelming sense of impending loss. He drew her tight to him, one hand gently holding her head against his chest, the other around her waist. He now controlled, comforted, protected her. He was now a man.

They lay close together all night and gently he told her the full story of his illness. When he had finished he held her tight, kissed her face. She looked at him through a mist of tears.

"David. I'm so afraid."

"No. Don't be darling. It will be alright," she lay quietly in his arms, thinking about his words.

"Judy......would you still love me if I was different? Different but still me."

"Of course I would," she squeezed him, felt him

stiffen so she turned to look into his eyes, saw how serious he was. "What exactly do you mean?"

"Well. What if I was younger?....I mean a lot younger. Would it make any difference to the way you feel about me?"

Her eyes misted over and she turned away, didn't say anything but just listened to him as he told her of his plans, of his meeting with Jonas, of how he planned his own rebirth.

Then she really became afraid. There was something wrong, something unnatural in what he planned to do. Judy became quiet, she didn't tell him of her fears, gave herself time to consider. She turned away from him with feigned yawn and allowed him to lay close to her, arm around her. She turned her head towards him and with closed eyes and puckered lips, kissed him gently before turning again to face the other way. With a wriggle she pushed close against his body.

"Night darling," she murmured.

She didn't fall asleep for a long time, lying with her back to him and her eyes closed, she allowed her mind to wander, take in all he had told her. David too lay in that hazy stage that somehow escapes the final entry into sleep, happy but unable to put his thoughts away.

Close to dawn, as Judy dwelt in that state of restlessness between sleep and consciousness, she dreamed. She dreamed of David's death, saw his spirit, his life force lift from his dying body and drift not into an unborn child but into the unconscious body of a naked man. He was strong, muscular, the physical opposite of David. In her dream she stood naked beside David's corpse, watched as his spirit rose from his body, just like David had described it to her after that first experiment. Then as the spirit lifted and moved, she followed it towards the man. As David's spirit sank into the prone form she bent over the man whose face seemed a blur, unformed. She leaned closer and her lips touched his. Suddenly she felt life where there had been none. His lips responded to hers, engulfed hers. Strong arms encircled her, pulling her towards him, crushing her body to his.

"No!" She screamed. "You're not David!"

She struggled, pushing her hands against his chest and forcing him away from her. His face was now crystal clear and laughing eyes looked at her possessively.

"No. No!" She screamed. The face wavered and was lost as she awoke panting. In its place she saw David lying beside her. Suddenly she felt ashamed, she felt she had to get away from him.

Judy got out of bed, wrapped a robe around herself and walked uncertainly into the other room. There she stopped, leaning back against a wall. She closed her eyes and wept silently.

"Oh God. Why? Why me?"

"Why Michael?"

STILLBORN

CHAPTER FOUR

Judy was becoming impatient. After all she had called David twice in the last hour to remind him that they were supposed to be meeting Michael and Hannah at nine o'clock. It was already ten past and still there was no sign of him. She was pacing up and down the room, glancing at the clock and becoming more annoyed by the minute. The last time she had phoned him half an hour earlier, he had been so engrossed in his work that his abstract confirmation that he was just about to leave did nothing to reassure her.

"Damn him!" She muttered, annoyed by his obsession with the project and his apparent lack of concern for her. There was nothing so infuriating as talking to someone, knowing they were only going through the motions of answering, while ninety percent of their attention was devoted to something else going on inside their head.

Forgetting his illness in her moment of anger, she asked herself what would he be like in ten or twenty years? When the excitement in their relationship had died down, would she only see this side of him? The annoying, inconsiderate person that perhaps he really was. 'Damn!' She cursed, 'why couldn't she have fallen for somebody more down to earth, more manly, someone like.......'

She stopped her pacing, shocked again that her thoughts had returned to Michael. Things seemed to be losing cohesion, it felt as if the order in her life was being eroded by events, by emotions. This had only happened since she and David had slept together. She momentarily stopped her pacing.

'Yes,' she said to herself. 'That was when it started!' She was being betrayed by these new feelings, her body seemed to be taking over control of her mind and it was all her own fault. She had instigated the whole thing. She had seduced David in the first place, kidding herself that her actions were because of her deep love and compassion for him, when really she was just satisfying her own carnal desires. Since that first night she had taken every opportunity to satisfy herself and David was so completely captivated by her that he hadn't offered the least resistance to her advances. She hadn't been to confession either, abandoning her church in the shame of her own selfish actions.

The question she now asked herself was, had this all happened because of her love for David, or was she merely satisfying her own needs and desires and was now being punished?

The phone rang and she walked over to the coffee table and picked it up, expecting to hear David's voice.

"Hi Judy. What are you two up to?"

"Oh... Michael. I thought it would be David, he's been held up but he won't be long. Shall we meet you there?"

"Give him another call first. If he can't get back in ten minutes tell him to meet us there. I'll come and pick you up."

"Are you sure? Hannah won't mind will she?"

"'course not. Call me back and let me know, OK?"

"Thanks Michael, I'll speak to you in a minute."

"Sure."

Immediately she put down the receiver it rang again. "Michael?"

STILLBORN

"It's David."

"David. Michael just called to find out what had happened to us, they were going to come and find us. Are you finished?"

"I'm sorry Judy, I'll be about half an hour. Why don't you go on with them? I'll join you there"

"Are you sure David? I feel mean going without you. I'll wait if you want me to"

"No, you go on. I promise I won't be long."

"Okay. See you soon darling."

She replaced the receiver and tried to suppress a feeling that was a mixture of relief and poorly disguised guilt. Relief that he had not insisted on her waiting for him and guilt that she wanted to go with Michael. Her last suggestion that she wait was not very sincere and, in truth, was uttered more for her own absolution than because she wanted things that way. She quickly telephoned Michael and told him the situation. He said they would be over to collect her in a few moments.

It was all so confusing and she did feel very bad about the way she was handling things. Poor David, she thought, he has so much on his mind with his work as well as his illness. No wonder he looks haggard.

Like most people who try to deny their true feelings even to themselves, it didn't last for long. She soon returned her attention to her own appearance. Looking into the mirror she was much more conscious than usual of the way she looked.

Fifteen minutes later when the doorbell rang she did her best to ignore the fluttering of her heart but on seeing him before her she became totally absorbed in the moment. At the same time she was annoyed with herself. She felt awkward and silly when she was alone in his presence, like some little girl about to go on her first date.

"Hi Judy, you look great. Hannah's waiting in the taxi so if you are ready?"

Michael held out an arm with mock courtesy and as he spoke Judy found herself captivated by the sound of his voice rather than the words he said. But eventually the words filtered through, she heard the name Hannah and blushed profusely.

"I'm ready Michael," she said demurely.

Judy didn't take the offered arm, pretending not to notice. As she walked before him she imagined she could feel that his eyes were appraising her as he followed.

Subconsciously perhaps, this pleased her and added something to her movements.

David was satisfied with the preparations so far. Time had flown since that initial breakthrough in the hospital, and being Thursday, four days had passed since his meeting with Jonas. Both Michael and he had concentrated all their energies on making the final analysis of the results from the tests on the first batch of reincarnated monkeys whose donors had been given the drug they had developed.

The tests were very simple. After the initial breakthrough and with the help of CDG's experimental drug laboratory, they had worked on the development of a drug that seemed it would promote memory retention after death. Having established the fact that the spirit existed in a magnetic form that carried a being's personal characteristics into a new life, they had decided to develop a drug that they hoped would firstly increase the volume of the spirit emission from the dying brain, and secondly, promote complete memory transfer utilising the additional 'memory' space within the spirit. Strangely the drug that they were using was a combination based on a formula that had shown remarkable success in the treatment of Alzheimer's disease added to a derivative of LSD, a hallucinogenic popular among 60's hippies.

The work had been slow but very rewarding and was based on further experiments that were carried out in the same way as the initial successful one but on monkeys instead of human guinea-pigs.

The only problem that had persisted was in containing the spirit within a chamber. During the first experiment David had thought the door that allowed the spirit to escape had been opened by a member of the hospital staff. However the sequence was repeated every time and somehow the spirit always managed to escape until the chamber had been modified in such a way that all exits were disabled and restrained mechanically from the inside. Then the spirit did not escape but after a five minute period in which the room seemed to be subjected to inexplicable forces, eerie flashes of white light and indescribable sounds and motion, the spirit simply evaporated.

David & Michael spent many sleepless nights considering this problem until they finally settled for an assumption that unless the spirit found a suitable recipient or "resting place" within about five minutes, then it simply died. The moral implications disturbed David because if all their theories were correct, individual spirits had existed in continuity since time began, passing from one life to another while that mortal form was able to sustain them. Their experimentation had interrupted that chain, and perhaps, caused the death of a life form that had been there for as long as man had existed.

Judy and he discussed this over and over while lying together at night and because they decided that it was wrong to halt the passage of a spirit in this way, all later experimentation allowed the escape of the spirit, unless there was a recipient within the chamber. It seemed that if the options were controlled, allowing a single recipient for a single departing spirit, then the spirit would be forced into accepting that choice. The results he had obtained that day were based on a program in which the monkeys were taught simple demand exercises. Press the right button and receive food for example. Having taught a group of monkeys several of these routines they were each put to sleep in a controlled sealed chamber with a recipient pregnant monkey which was within one week of giving birth.

This element of timing proved to be essential, although it had been arrived at through trial and error. As they did not know at what stage of its development the foetus or child was capable of receiving a spirit, early experiments involved the necessity of having several monkeys at different stages of their pregnancy within the chamber at the time of the "donor's" death. The results showed that the transfer was only successful within about one week of birth and an off shoot of the experiments provided medical research with some very good material in understanding an age old mental disorder that had eluded them. It seemed that more than one spirit could occupy the same being, therefore transferring more than one character into one body. This allowed the development of a being with a split or double personality, a condition more commonly known as schizophrenia. David rubbed his eyes and looked up from the papers in front of him. He was pleased with what they had achieved, things had gone well. Then a frown replaced the glimmer of a smile as he suddenly remembered how little time there was left and how much more he had to accomplish during the coming months; preparation of a suitable facility for a human transfer experiment, plenty of checking and double checking of the new drug, testing for side-effects, ensuring they had the correct doses. Lastly and of particular interest to David, was the job of selecting the right recipient for his own transfer.

It was a unique and fascinating prospect, the choosing of his own parents.

He shook himself as if to ward off the fear that came when he considered this. The final stage in his program was acceptable when it was viewed in a purely scientific way. Sometimes he couldn't help thinking about the very personal aspects, the administration of the drug, the experience of his own death, his rebirth, the restrictions imposed by years of physical and perhaps mental infancy.

As he thought of himself as a child again he realised how difficult it would be for Judy. While she was a mature woman, the David she knew would have inherited a new and unfamiliar body. Would she love him still when he became a child again, inherited a child's body, a child's mind...perhaps even its emotions?

Would she wait?

As he thought of her he suddenly became aware of the time. He guiltily remembered where he should be and for once his loyalty to Judy and his friends over-

came his absorption in his work. He had said he would
be there half an hour earlier. Hurriedly he tidied his
desk and interrupted the program before closing down
the computer.

The restaurant they had chosen was an exact repro-
duction of one situated on an island in the Seine, in
the centre of Paris. It carried the original name, "Les
Ancestoirs du Gauloise." If a Parisian had stepped
through the door into this copy of his favourite eating place, he would hardly have known the difference. Only the fact that the customers predominantly
spoke English and were perhaps more reserved in their
mannerisms could have possibly exposed the fraud.
Judy, Hannah and Michael were shown to the only
vacant table in the crowded room that was already
buzzing with conversation and laughter. In the same
way as the others there, the three were well dressed
for the evening. The restaurant was considered chic
and the patrons were attired accordingly. A small
ensemble were tucked away discreetly in a dark al-
cove and played traditional french music of a bygone
age, adding to the authenticity of the illusion.
Judy's mood lightened as they soaked up the gaiety
around them and she smiled at Hannah and Michael
and looking at him suggested a drink.
"Lets have some wine Michael. I'd like the red it
seems more French somehow. Le vin rouge s'il vous
plait"
"Certainment mademoiselle, et tu Hannah?"
"D'accord monsieur. Le vin rouge, c'est parfait".
They all laughed as Michael rose and made his way
to the huge barrels in a corner of the room where he
selected a large carafe and filled it from the tap. As

soon as he was out of ear-shot, Judy and Hannah started chatting about the restaurant and the other people there. Their conversation was centred mainly around the way others were dressed, guessing who they were and trying to unravel what information they could from the glances and gestures of the other women. Every now and then they would pick up a snippet of conversation on which they could expand. Michael was soon back with the wine which he poured with a flourish while commenting on the hors d'oeuvres he had seen on display. The particular theme of this restaurant, in keeping with its counterpart in Paris, was that the guests helped themselves to as much wine and food as they wanted from the huge barrels and refectory tables heaped with hors d'oeuvres. The main courses were served by the waitresses but the constant movement of diners around the room added to the relaxed and friendly atmosphere.

"The garlic prawns and the champignons with Roquefort cheese smell fantastic. But I'm going to start with escargots."

"Urgh that's revolting," said Hannah with conviction. "Can you imagine people actually eating such revolting, slimy little things as snails."

"Oh I don't know. We ate all sorts at home when I was a child, raw fish, sea slug."

"Michael! Some of the customs you inherited from your grandfather are so primitive."

"Come on Hannah. Surely that's part of the reason why you married me, because of the animal in me!"

Judy felt herself growing annoyed with Hannah's coquettishness, particularly as it was in censure of Michael. She quickly changed the subject. The reaction did not go unnoticed by the attentive Michael.

"I wonder when David's going to get here? I'm starving."

"Lets wait another ten minutes then start on the hors d'oeuvres. David probably wouldn't notice if we had gorged and drunk ourselves into a stupor. He's always so wrapped up in his work."

"That's not fair Hannah." said Judy immediately jumping to David's defence. "He's got a lot on his mind at the moment."

"That's right Hannah. He's been hard at it lately. We both have," added Michael, apparently also speaking up for David but subconsciously in support of Judy. "Its true though. At least you know when to switch off Michael. It takes an awful lot to get David's mind off his work."

"If you can't do that Judy, then nobody can." Again as Michael spoke Judy felt the blood rising to her cheeks but she was saved from any further embarrassement as she spotted David being led through the room to their table. He hadn't even changed. He had come straight from the laboratory and his drab appearance stood out as he walked, head bent, towards them.

"Hi David!"

As soon as he heard Judy's voice his head lifted and a smile came to his face. Judy was reassured to feel that warm glow of pleasure that his smile brought her..

"Sorry darling. I got here as quickly as possible." He bent forward and kissed Judy gently on the lips.

"Hope you haven't started without me. Hi Hannah, happy birthday."

"Yes. Let's drink to Hannah," commanded Judy,

raising her glass.

Michael leant over and filled David's glass before raising his own.

"Happy birthday Hannah."

They each drank, toasting Hannah and giving their individual greetings.

Soon the conversation returned to other matters.

"Did you complete the tests?" Michael asked, turning to David.

"Come on boys. No talking shop tonight. I'm surprised at you," interrupted Hannah.

"Ok, Ok.... Shall we get some food?" Asked Michael.

"You three carry on. The main course will be enough for me. I'm really not that hungry."

"I'll stay with David, I'm on another diet."

Michael rose from his seat and turned to Judy and with an elaborate bow and that mischievous smile he held out his hand to her.

"Veux tu m'accompagne, mademoiselle?"

"Merci monsieur," Judy offered her hand delicately to Michael and rose with exaggerated elegance. All four of them broke into laughter again as the couple walked away from the table.

"Hey, you really look great tonight Judy. I think you would be completely at home in Paris."

"Thanks. You make a pretty good courtier yourself."

"Judy?" He turned and looked into her eyes.

"Yes?"

He placed a hand lightly on her shoulder and spoke softly, seriously.

"I've been hoping we would get a chance to be on our own. We need to talk about what's happening to David? You know..... I mean he has told you, hasn't he?"

Judy stopped as they reached the hors d'oeuvres and half turned towards Michael letting her hand fall gently on to his forearm.

"I don't know how much David has told you but I'm going to go crazy unless I talk to someone."

"Talk to me then Judy. I'm as worried as you are," he was very serious, the playful smile had left his face, his eyes glowed but it was with intent, the humour had gone.

Suddenly he felt conspicuous because of their seriousness. A glance over his shoulder told him that David was unaware, he and Hannah were chatting away and not paying them any attention. Nevertheless he let go of Judy and turned back to the table. He picked up a plate which he started to fill with food, not noticing what he was taking.

Suddenly they were oblivious to the room, caught in their own little world, very conscious of each other. But they misinterpreted the feelings that were causing their seriousness and intensity. They confused them with their shared concern for David. Their mutual desire was interpreted as sadness over David's illness.

Distractedly, Michael loaded his plate with a few snails, some beluga caviar and french bread. With a slightly trembling hand he popped a cracker with mayonnaise and anchovy into his mouth.

"David's dying!" Her face almost collapsed in tears and Michael all but spat out the cracker and erupted into a coughing fit as the food went the wrong way. Her sudden outburst surprised him, instantly bringing the reality of David's death into focus. He put his plate down and slowly turned towards her. Reaching out a hand he took her arm as if to comfort her.

STILLBORN

"Judy!" He looked at her, all humour gone from his eyes now.

"No Michael, not here. Please. I have to talk to someone and now I know that you know as well, it had better be with you. Anyway I can't think of anyone I would trust more than you. You've always been such a good friend to David..." As he looked into her eyes and saw the tears form he felt that old knot form in his stomach and he just wanted to reach out and pull her into his arms.

"Ok Judy....... they will be wondering what is going on with the two of us. I'll meet you tomorrow at your place. Twelve-thirty, take an early lunch," he squeezed her arm, forcing her to look at him. "It may not be as bad as you think...I mean David...oh shit! Lets get some food."

"Yes." She wiped the tears away from her eyes, forcing out a laugh to contradict their existence. Judy took the plate Michael handed her and picked up a few pieces but really her appetite had gone. The last few days had been like this all the time since David had told her of his illness. Then there was the emotional upheaval that followed their love making. As Michael turned to lead the way back she gazed at his dark hair and broad shoulders and muttered.

"Oh yes it is. Worse than you can imagine".

The rest of the evening was a bit of an effort for everybody. Hannah always seemed slightly ill at ease in company being a bit of an introvert, which was obviously in stark contrast to Michael's flamboyant nature. David was tired and over worked and perhaps his illness and the drugs were taking their toll. He was never exactly the life and soul of a party.

The two extroverts, Michael and Judy, were noticeably quieter than usual, seemingly lost in their own thoughts for long periods. When Judy looked up from time to time, she would see a quiet half smile on Michael's face. Aware of her unhappiness, he did his best to reassure her. Sometimes she would catch him as well, pondering his own problems, an inquisitive expression in his eyes as if he was wrestling with a problem that had been bothering him for some time. Which, of course, he was. Something had happened. Suppressed feelings had made their way to the surface of his mind. He analysed his own reaction to the news about David and particularly how he felt about Judy.

He had known her for only a few months, since she first became involved with David. As he let his mind drift, he remembered their first meeting clearly and the first time that he had looked into her eyes. He knew he was attracted to her but had always disregarded this feeling as being that of any hot blooded male when meeting a very attractive woman.

Michael struggled to keep the evening alive by refilling everybody's glass as soon as it was half empty and cracking a few jokes. But all four of them were glad when David said he had an interview with Jonas early the next morning and must get some sleep. By the time they did leave Judy was quite merry again as a result of the wine of which she had really had a bit too much. David had his arm around her as they said their goodbyes. Hannah and Michael boarded the first taxi after the two women hugged and promised a shopping trip in the near future. David pecked Hannah's cheek while Michael enshrouded Judy in his usual bear hug while he whispered in an unusually gentle voice.

STILLBORN

"See you tomorrow. Try not to worry."

As the door closed and the taxi pulled away from the kerb, Judy and David waved briefly and then turned to the next one for their short journey home.

Once back at Judy's place David put his arms around her to begin the new pre bed ritual they had become used to.

Unexpectedly, Judy felt she wanted to be alone and placed her forefinger gently on David's lips.

"Not tonight darling. We're both exhausted and need a good night's rest. It's very late and don't forget your meeting with Jonas in the morning."

David didn't protest. He was indeed tired, it had been another very long day.

"Ok Judy. I'll see you tomorrow night. I shouldn't be late for a change."

"Good night David."

"Good night Judy. I love you."

"Me too," yawned Judy.

After he left, Judy let her clothes drop around her and stepped naked into bed. Briefly she reviewed the evening, thought about her conversation with Michael, the meeting they had arranged for the next day.

A smile passed over her face.

Thanks to the wine she was soon fast asleep and fell into the secret world of dreams which had recently been violent and confusing. But tonight, for a change, they were peaceful and she slept right through until the morning.

CHAPTER FIVE

The chairman of the board of CDG Pharmaceuticals was John Chapman. At seventy one he wasn't the oldest member, the average being well over the normal age of retirement that was permitted for shop floor staff and non-executive management.

Unlike most of the board members, John had at least earned his post, having worked his way up through the industry and acquiring on the way a reputation as a shrewd and energetic businessman. Like most British companies, several of the other directors had obtained their seat because of who they knew, not what they knew. Social position and wealth still scored points in the British board room.

CDG was a multinational, one of the few that was still controlled from inside Britain. Its autonomous position was continually under threat on the stock market and it wasn't without some vision by its leader that the company avoided a take over. To maintain its independence such a company had to be continually on the move. If it relied on steady turnover and high profits from its mainstream drug and cosmetics sectors, the vultures would strike. Its competitors, mainly US conglomerates, would attempt a take over. Through expansion and reinvestment, the company was continually increasing its share capital and spreading the risk of an attack on its stock through the diversity and volatility of the individual share holdings. At the same time, reinvestment of profits in acquisitions and research and development would prevent the company's balance sheet from appearing to be top heavy, its assets and net profits not so high and therefore a less attractive target.

John had led the company well. He had shown considerable flair in acquisitions and R&D projects were both innovative and diverse. It was because of this approach that he had managed to persuade the board to sanction the research being carried out by David Hawkin. Psychic research interested John. He had read a considerable amount on the subject of reincarnation and theology generally and the possibility of an after-life was something he did not dismiss out of hand.

He was getting older too and with the advancement of years there came a subtle shift in his values. Material gain was of less importance, his semi-beliefs became more firm, his vested interest in an after-life more resolute.

David Hawkin's paper on reincarnation had attracted much interest within the scientific world. John Chapman, through his position as chairman of the CDG board, had indirectly set himself up as David's sponsor. It hadn't been too difficult to persuade the other board members to increase R&D funds for this project. Apart from any potential long term profits that the company may benefit from, the newspapers had made much of their funding this unusual field of research. The publicity had temporarily increased public awareness of CDG and share prices had jumped a few points.

But all that had been six months ago. The media no longer showed much interest in David Hawkin's research but expenditure continued and was even rising.

Then there was the state of the economy globally which had a considerable bearing on today's meeting. The current recession had hit CDG shares quite badly. To make things worse, Leisure Investments Ltd., a capital intensive subsidiary of CDG, had 'gone under'. When it was announced that it had ceased trading a few days earlier, CDG shares had dropped considerably.

John wasn't too worried by all this, he knew that to some extent you had 'to go with the flow'. The key to success was to stay one step ahead, be flexible and even do an about turn if necessary.

At this special meeting the auditors had been brought in and their results and forecasts had been dissected and disseminated. The mood of the board was negative, they wanted cuts, cost savings. John himself favoured digging in, pursuing their objectives. Certainly re-evaluate, perhaps restructure where necessary, but his personal policy was to fight the current market depression with flair not fear.

To some extent he knew he had to placate the board and that was his intent at the moment, to lead them into a belief that he was meeting their demands but at the same time safeguarding his own objectives.

"The point is," he said. "Expenditure in your department has risen steeply over the last few months. I shouldn't have to remind you of your responsibility to contain the use of resources within the agreed budget."

Twelve sets of eyes homed in on Jonas, each adopting the same accusatory expression that was projected in the chairman's voice.

Jonas sighed to himself, fully aware that his position was under continual scrutiny. Regardless of the fact that his department had achieved some outstanding results over the past few years, there were still sceptics. As he thought about his reply, he looked at the venomous expressions on the faces of the old men who were inspecting him. Somehow he managed to hide the contempt that he felt. In his eyes they were stuffed shirts who through their own ignorance treated his department with doubt and looked on his work as fantasy and those involved as dreamers rather than scientists. But he also knew that if he could pull the wool over their eyes for a little while longer, such incidentals as increased expenditure would be forgotten amid the acclaim that he would receive when he published the results of David's experiments.

For Jonas it was a two sided game, with him in the middle like a referee, mediating, encouraging, placating. On one side there was David who he had to keep motivated with vague promises of his future while on the other team were the board from whom he had to hide the real reason for the increased expenditure.

Obviously he couldn't tell them the truth. Firstly they wouldn't believe him and secondly they were so stuck in their ways that they wouldn't commit the necessary resources to what they would negatively perceive to be an outside chance of success.

Jonas didn't really care about the project, David or these silly old men. The truth was that he had made progress through the hierarchy of the company by taking chances, by having the vision to proceed along a course that nobody else would dare to follow. All that really concerned him was that the success of the program would earn him a seat on this board, a position which he felt he undoubtedly deserved. In turn that surely would enable him to take over as chairman within a very short time. Jonas Nichols would become the youngest chairman of the CDG's board in its history and with the power that it would give him he could soon move onto the political ladder where his real expertise would come to the fore.

In the meantime his task was to soft soap the board to obtain the necessary funds. For this he was fully prepared.

"John..... There are another six months before the financial year end when the board will seek ratification and you will rightly be re-elected."

He paused to allow the inevitable murmurs of agreement.

"Its unfortunate that this surge in expenditure occurred before the end of the last quarter or you would never have seen it. The fact is that although my department is presently spending over budget, it will have operated below its planned level when the full year's accounts are prepared!"

That's better he thought as he saw a few of the expressions relax. Now for the punch-line.

"Gentlemen," he boomed "I am expecting a breakthrough with the new drug we have been working on for the treatment of Alzheimer's disease."

Repressing a smirk, he thought to himself, 'Might be useful to a few of you'.

"The results will amount to a breakthrough in the treatment of this disease. Demand worldwide will be enormous!"

Jonas smiled broadly and let his eyes travel from one face to another while trying to read each man's reactions as he did so. Certainly the whole atmosphere of the meeting had relaxed and they were all hanging on his words. The new drug had been under development for several years now and R&D had been very costly, the end results always uncertain.

The fact that Jonas knew it was a flop was beside the point as far as he was concerned. What could it do anyway? He asked himself. Dilute senility in old men like these for a few more years, enable the brain to outlast decrepit and decaying bodies! Humpff! It would never have the emotive effect that eternal life could bring and surely consciousness through death and rebirth amounted to that. Every being that existed would want it. He, Jonas Nichols, would control it!

The problem he had at this moment was to raise the necessary funds without letting them know what he really wanted them for. Not yet, he thought. Not until he had absolute control. And that was only a matter of time. After all the only three people who would be privy to the details of the process would be David Hawkin, his assistant Tamasoto and Jonas himself. Well, he mused, David wouldn't be around to collect the rewards and the other one, the foreigner. Well Jonas would deal with that problem when the time came.

Looking into their eyes he knew he had them eating out of his hands. All that remained was the final push. He let his smile drop and adopted a serious attitude, then as he spoke again he added a tinge of disappointment and humility to his voice.

"The additional resources are only necessary in completing that program. Unfortunately my department does not have any other major projects on the drawing board and it will therefore be necessary to reduce staff and cut the size of the entire department.....perhaps even consider closure altogether."

As his oration tailed off he saw their expressions change. A few smiles of self satisfaction and smugness appeared on their faces. He laughed inwardly. He knew that they despised him and that his calculated show of humble surrender would be seized upon.

'Fools!' He thought.' Just look at their expressions. Puppets. I pull the right strings and they dance my tune.'

It was all he could do to lower his head in mock humility. Inside he was filled with self adulation, pride at his ability to control them. With an effort he suppressed the laughter rising in his chest...'my day will come,' he mused. 'Then we will see who calls the tune.'

He was saved any further acts of self-denigration as one of his greatest adversaries rose to his feet, demanding the board's attention.

"Gentlemen. I'm sure the board will join me in expressing our thanks to Jonas for his candidness," he turned towards the recipient of his gloating. '... and in sharing my disappointment over the future of his department. I propose we accede to his request for additional support over the short term. I am sure that I speak for all the members of the board in expressing my hope that his department can continue its useful contributions in albeit a...ahem... reduced capacity." The last few words were delivered in mock sincerity and accompanied by a condescending smile but the satisfaction felt by the speaker was nothing compared to that felt by Jonas. Somehow however, the big man managed to hide his true feelings behind a suitably contrite expression.

Mumbles of agreement and muted expressions of

commiseration followed from the other board members until they were brought to a timely end by the back to business attitude of a relieved chairman.

"All those in favour of approving the request for additional short term resources for Mr Nichols's department?"

"Aye" Twelve voices uttered in unison.

"Against?"

Silence.

"Thank you Jonas, your request is approved and we look forward with some anticipation to the results of your current program."

"Thank you John," said Jonas humbly, then turning to face the other members, added. "I would like to thank the entire board for their support. I can assure you all that your confidence has not been misplaced." A smile crept on to Jonas's face but with an effort he managed to stop it turning into a full blooded laugh.

"Thank you Jonas. That will be all," said John Chapman in a dismissive way. Then turning towards the table and without paying any obvious attention to Jonas's departure he continued with the rest of the day's business.

"Now gentlemen. The next matter on the agenda involves the question of liquidating Leisure Investments Ltd."

Jonas stood up and left the room discreetly without attracting any more attention. Only John Chapman, who was perhaps more astute than Jonas allowed, watched him leave and allowed a moments uncertainty to show in his eyes. Just for a brief moment the question crossed his mind, 'had they been fooled?' Then as the door closed behind him so these misgivings subsided as his attention was brought back to the matters in hand. Outside the door Jonas could not contain the smile that caused the edges of his mouth to curl and his eyes to sparkle. As he shuffled his huge frame out of earshot it turned into a laugh.

Judy had not enjoyed the morning at all. Waking up she had a stale taste in her mouth from the night before and that unsettled feeling that comes from too much alcohol. She felt irritable from the first moment of consciousness when she had been awakened by her alarm. Everything seemed more difficult to do or tedious in its doing, even the simple chores of preparing for the day. She had no appetite and had skipped her usual breakfast, just taking a warm drink before leaving for CDG.

Work was impossible. It demanded a lot of concentration, a commodity she seemed to have run out of and she was annoyed with herself when half way through whatever she tried to do she would find her mind wandering and filling with questions. Questions concerning David and Michael and her own feelings that she seemed unable to control. Memories of the recent and wonderful feelings that she had evoked with David seemed to be interlaced with the attraction that she undoubtedly felt for Michael and that for some silly reason had sprung to the surface only recently. As she thought about this she unconsciously compared the two men, their personalities, their nature, their physiques. The blue eyes and dark hair and skin, the slightly oriental set of his eyes adding mystery. Michael was certainly attractive. Tall and broad shouldered, he emanated strength and vigour in the way he stood and moved. Perhaps, she thought, that was why she was attracted to him. Just a pure animal fascination. Then there was poor David. Certainly no match for Michael in a physical sense, but then it wasn't his appearance, his stature, that Judy had fallen for. It was after all his mind that had first attracted her to him and this initial attraction had indeed blossomed so that she felt a need to be close to him, to protect him. Possibly, she thought, it was her feelings for David that were based on the wrong instincts. Perhaps the closeness and warmth she felt were maternal while the attraction she felt for Michael was what she should feel for a man.

Damn! She cursed herself inwardly. Again she attempted to block her thoughts and concentrate on her work but it was just no use. She took a break, sat at a table on her own in a corner of the canteen nursing a cup of coffee and lost in thought until someone disturbed her and she remembered to go back to work.

Then the whole disconcerting process would start over again. Finally she gave up and signed out with an excuse of feeling unwell. She made her way as quickly as she could back to the privacy of her apartment where she could be alone with her feelings.

It was an hour before her arranged meeting with Michael and she lay on the couch and gave into her thoughts. She surrendered consciously, hoping that if she came face to face with her emotions, then perhaps she could understand them and come to terms with the situation.

She stretched out comfortably and let her mind wander back over recent events. She thought about David's illness and tried to assess how she felt about it. She hadn't cried, not even while she was alone. She had used the news as an excuse to allow herself

free rein in exercising her own sexual desires with
the self deception that she was helping David through
his grief. Having done so, she seemed to have opened
up a hornet's nest of destructive emotions.

Her thoughts travelled on to Michael in an attempt to
analyse the way she felt about him. She knew he was
attractive but that in itself made little sense to her.
After all, she had known him for several months and
his physical appearance had not aroused any dramatic
feelings in the past. He was just Michael, David's
friend and colleague and he should have remained just
that. It was more than straight forward desire, it was
not just his physical appearance that attracted her
now. It was those extra qualities that none of her other
friends shared. Michael had an attractive character
that complemented his appearance and he was good
humoured, attentive, kind and understanding. Above
all he was somehow more human, more real.

She realised that she liked him. Really liked him. She
was not too certain as to whether she could say the
same about David. She guessed Michael was also very
perceptive, he seemed able to pick up on other
people's moods and feelings quickly. Then there were
his eyes. For a moment she let herself visualise those
blue, secretive eyes that sparkled when he laughed.
They were strange, blue Western eyes that somehow
still held the mystery of the East.

She stopped her self-analysis, shut down her feelings.
'God!' She cursed. 'What am I doing?..... I love David
not Michael!'

Judy got up from the couch and went into the
bathroom where she splashed water on her face in an
attempt to clear her thoughts. She looked up into the
mirror and saw the strained expression on her face

and almost unconsciously she began to prepare herself for the meeting with Michael.

In some respects she wished that she had never agreed to see him but as she had, she decided that she would keep it as short and unemotional as possible. Michael had caught her at a weak moment the previous evening but now she had her feelings under more control. She would just tell him she was sorry for wasting his time and get it over with as quickly as possible.

Nevertheless, and without realising it, she spent the next fifteen minutes paying more attention to her appearance than she would normally have done. She took a long shower and carefully selected the clothes that emphasised the more attractive aspects of her appearance. As the appointed time drew closer she felt more and more apprehension that she tried without success to ignore.

The knock on the door, so sudden, so unexpected, surprised Judy. At the same time its import was clear to her. With a last glance in the mirror and a quick corrective flick of her hair she turned and hurried anxiously to open the door.

Michael too had that strange sense of anxiety that usually precedes an illicit sexual liaison. Not that he felt the arranged meeting with Judy had any deceitful undertones, he was after all David's friend as well as hers and it was only because of his concern for them both and to try to help, that he had agreed to meet her.

As he sat on the tube he tried to rationalise his feelings of guilt. The rhythm of the train lulled him into a temporary state of well being and he looked back at the beginning of his relationship with

Hannah.

He had met her soon after his arrival in England and only three months later they were married. It wasn't exactly a whirlwind love affair, Michael was lonely and didn't know many people and Hannah was an undemanding and undemonstrative woman who fell quietly in love with him. She was the type of woman who needed a man, who only felt happy when she had a broad shoulder to lean on, someone to trust and believe in. Michael was strong, he was the type of person you could rely upon while at the same time he was imaginative and very kind.

Michael also knew himself well and accepted his own sexuality as part of his character. Throughout school and later at college his athletic prowess had set him up as the target for many girls. Before leaving home he had several encounters with a variety of women and enjoyed them both sexually and socially. He was the type of man who preferred the company of women to that of men and had been fortunate in this respect, always having had plenty of opportunity to mix with women.

Coming to England had been a turning point in his life. After the death of his grandfather he lost the comfort of a close family around him and he had arrived in a society where his expertise in American football meant nothing.

For the first time in his life he had been lonely.

His relationship with Hannah was good, not earth moving but solid. He did not look at other women and did not consider the possibility of becoming involved with anyone else even if the opportunity arose. If asked he would have considered that he was well equipped for a long term relationship having at least sown his wild oats as a young man. Of course, if he had given it more consideration, he may have come to the conclusion that having experienced sexual freedom he would find it difficult to accept the rigid guidelines that long term monogamy required.

Even if he had admitted to himself that he was attracted to Judy, there was nothing he could do about it. He was married and Judy was out of reach, she was engaged to his best friend. That was something he accepted. Certainly he admired her and was fully aware that he found her attractive. He enjoyed being with her and felt the vibrance that she gave out and the excitement she created within him. When sharing her company it seemed as if he were a smouldering fire that somehow she magically caused to ignite. If he had given it enough thought he would also have realised that Judy held for him that magic quality that made him feel more of a man.

It was with some surprise that he became aware of a feeling of acute nervousness as he made his way to Judy's apartment. He felt that anticipatory dread form like a knot in his stomach and did his very best to deny what he knew he was feeling. He stepped up to her door and hesitated, then taking a deep breath he raised his right hand in a fist and tapped lightly on her door.

David hadn't gone straight into the laboratory that morning for a meeting with Jonas as he had told the others. Instead he was at the Harley Street rooms of an eminent physician, one with a high reputation in the treatment of cancers. He didn't know why he had lied or why he hadn't told Judy that he was seeing another doctor. Perhaps it was out of fear of disappointment that this last ditch effort would be useless.

Jonas had used his influence to arrange this consultation with Dr James Bruce. David had seen him briefly before being subjected to a series of further tests.

Now he was about to be given this man's verdict.

Sitting there waiting he was surprised that he had taken an instant dislike to Dr Bruce. He felt annoyed at what he perceived was the man's unnecessary arrogance and that it should exist in a person with such a high reputation.

"The doctor will see you now, Professor Hawkin."

Even the receptionist's voice seemed to have acquired a tone of aloofness. The medical profession are all the same, thought David. They get carried away with the power of life and death that they hold over their patients.

A door opened and a nurse looked at David.

"Thank you," he said testily and followed the nurse into a lavish office where Dr Bruce was sitting behind an extra large desk scanning some print-outs.

"Be seated." Not even a please or a look of recognition.

David was a mild mannered man in normal circumstances but once aroused he could become quite cutting and could use his intellect to destroy the arguments of a less well equipped person.

"Ahem?"

No response. "

Dr.?"

"Just wait a minute. Can't you see I'm busy", the doctor didn't raise his eyes as he spoke. He coughed into his hand, in the way some do when they are irritated.

Then he carried on reading.

"You are not the only person in this room with a back-log of work. The longer you keep me sitting here the more I have to catch up on when I can finally get back to it!"

"Ahem..yes, you've made your point, er Mr....", the condescending remark was accompanied by an annoyed wave of his hand. Dr Bruce shuffled through a pile of files to find the appropriate one belonging to the current 'nuisance' sitting the other side of his desk. Sometimes he wondered why he had chosen such a profession. He always seemed to be surrounded by fools and people intent on distracting him. 'Really!' He muttered to himself, 'Some people.'

"Professor Hawkin!" Corrected David, becoming even more annoyed.

"Oh yes. Yes, er forgive me professor. I was just looking for your test results."

The attempt at an apology was accompanied by an unexpected blush. Dr Bruce obviously did not deal with many patients with such an elevated title as his own and his attitude was probably corrected by a fleeting memory of being disciplined by some long forgotten tyrant of a professor while at medical school.

"I think you will find the results you are looking for in that green file on your left."

"Oh yes. Thank you professor."

Dr Bruce picked up the culprit file and scanned through the computer print-outs, the results of the tests David had undergone that morning. After some thought he decided to adopt his man to man attitude. Leaning back in his chair and looking David straight in the eyes, he began speaking in what he considered to be both a suitably sombre and forthright tone.

"You know the position professor, so I won't beat around the bush. You are in remission at the moment but the disease is at an advanced stage. Cancerous cells are present in major organs. The prognosis is poor. I can hopefully sustain you in your present condition for about six or seven months but the effect of the high doses of the drugs used to control pain and prevent too much physical deterioration will begin to have a severe toxic effect. I'm sorry but there is little further I can do apart from prescribing the same treatment," he paused to allow this to sink in. "You have six or seven, possibly eight months at the outside. After that I'm afraid its Hobson's choice. Either the disease kills you or the drugs do. I would suggest, in the circumstances, that you stop working immediately and enjoy the time you have left," he paused and adjusted the gold rimmed bifocals. "I can recommend a very good hospice. I believe they have everything there for your comfort. Highly trained staff. Oh...are you receiving counselling?"

David bit his lip in an effort to control his anger. Anger not only at this irritating man but also at the disease and the fates that had put him in this position.

"Thank you for your candour and advice doctor. I don't need a hospice or counselling. I came to you for time. I'm involved in a most sensitive and delicate project which is nearing completion. It is essential that I am able to continue my work for as long as possible."

Dr Bruce glanced up at David, deciding to pay more attention to the man behind the patient. Beneath the doctor's pompousness there was a sharp mind when he chose to apply it and David's words gave him cause to look at this man a little more closely. He saw in front of him a slightly dishevelled little man whose appearance would definitely not stand out in a crowd. But the voice, the air of authority and the intensity in the professor's expression, demanded more than lip service. He dropped his normal air of condescension and spoke forthrightly.

"There is a way we can extend your period of activity but there will be a price to pay. I can play a balancing game with the drugs, reduce the pain control, increase the cancer controlling drugs. The reduction in toxicity this produces will allow me to increase the stimulants in order to maintain your faculties at a higher level. A reduction in the pain controlling agents will also reduce the stress on your heart, liver and kidneys and diminish the overall toxic effect. But the question you have to ask yourself is, are you prepared to work on through increasing discomfort? The pain will be severe at times."

"I'm in your hands doctor. Just give me as much time as possible. Nine months to a year should be sufficient. I'll live with the problems."

The two men looked at each other, initial dislike turned around into the beginnings of mutual respect.

"Ok professor. I will have your prescription ready at reception. Collect it on the way out. If things get too difficult call me," he picked up a card and scribbled on it. "My home number is on the back."

"Thank you doctor."

David rose to leave. Reaching the door he hesitated as he heard the doctor speak once again.

"Good luck professor".

Judy hesitated before opening the door, taking in a deep breath and firming her resolve. This was a mistake, she decided. Her problems were her own and if she needed to share them then it should be with David.

On the other side of the door Michael was equally bemused, half hoping that Judy wouldn't be there. The door opened and he was looking into her lovely eyes. He could have sworn he saw a tear form.

Judy opened the door and looked straight into his kind, humorous, solid face and those sparkling blue eyes and her resolve collapsed into a well of confusion. She knew she would cry and couldn't help herself.

He saw her expression crumble. The tears started to fall down her cheeks and she looked so lost and helpless. He stepped forward, unable to prevent his arms from going around her, powerless to prevent his face touching hers, feeling, tasting the salt tears and the trembling of her body.

He brought his arms around her and she did nothing to prevent it. She didn't know why she was crying but she couldn't stop the tears now streaming down her cheeks. She couldn't quell the sobs that came between breaths so she just clung to him feeling the comforting warmth of his face touching hers. She knew he was tasting the salt of her tears and she wanted ....more, much more. Her lips parted against his cheek. They slowly turned towards each other, her mouth hungrily searching for his, tasting first her own tears then the moistness of his mouth. She clung to him, tasted him, felt the hardness of his body against hers and became oblivious to everything. She just wanted him closer, much closer.

As her lips touched his, he felt a deep longing, a feeling that seemed to have been within him all his life waiting for this moment to erupt. Very gently he grasped her upper arms and pushed her away from him so that he could look into her face. He felt no shame or guilt and saw none in her eyes but he saw the light that danced within them and he felt as if he was drowning in a pool of emotion that he never knew existed.

She turned and let her hand drop to his and together they moved as if in a dream through the unreality of the living room into her bedroom. Their coming together held no similarity to the first time she had been with David, when she had controlled and directed the scenes. Here, instead, it was a mutually fulfilling experience. Neither needed to instigate their love making. Their mutual desire and that wonderful feeling of wanting and being wanted, a unique evenness filling them both with joy. Joy of giving and receiving, of loving and being loved. Of needing and being desired. But at the same time their juxtaposition was so right, his manliness, her femininity, complementing and fulfilling each other's needs.

Silently save for the sounds of their breathing they undressed. Never taking their eyes from each other until they stood totally naked, unashamedly looking at each other's beauty. Then slowly his arms came around her again and he drew her close to him and gently kissed her face, his hands wanting to explore her body but afraid to move in case, unwittingly, his actions would destroy the perfection of the moment. Tentatively he laid her on the bed and coming down beside her they turned to engulf each other in kisses, enjoying the closeness of their bodies which felt so necessary, so perfect and so incredibly new. He lay half on his back and half on his side facing her, his legs apart with one of hers between them and he pulled her close to him so that her face lay against his shoulder and he could look into her eyes. When he spoke it was in a different voice to the one she usually associated with him, gone was the humour, his eyes were wide and soft, full of caring, his voice gentle and melodic but throaty and masculine.

"Judy, I can't make love. Not now."

The way he said this was so innocent and without shame that it only accentuated his strengths and his masculinity. That he recognised his fears and allowed her to see his true self, his sensitivity, only increased her respect for him as a man.

She smiled at him and reaching up kissed his lips tenderly.

"It really doesn't matter Michael."

"But I want you to know why. I want to tell you how perfect this feels and how afraid I am."

"Its the same for me. I didn't mean this to happen but there was nothing I could have done to prevent it."

They talked for what seemed an eternity. Words came bubbling from their mouths, secrets they had never shared with anyone were exposed unashamedly. They told each other of their desires, their hopes, their fears. They exchanged opinions, views; knowing they would be understood, reciprocated. They smiled and laughed uncontrollably until their facial muscles ached from the very joy of being together. So much happiness and joy seemed to well up from the simplest exchange. The rightness of each other's skin and smell seemed to belie the fact that this was totally new. Where they touched, the touch was natural, super sensitive but accustomed. Their eyes took in every detail, each minutiae of expression or imported meaning. Great areas of their memories were wiped clean and suddenly filled with the imprint of each other. As if what was, had been forever.

While they talked their awareness of their nudity was pushed back from the forefront of their consciousness, taking second place to their desire to speak and listen on this new, intimate level. With the burden of self consciousness lifted from him, his erection returned; somehow, almost without meaning it to happen, he penetrated her and felt an incredible warmth envelope his body as he held her even closer. Suddenly, words disappeared as they gasped in unison, each feeling the joy of their closeness.

They didn't make love for long or with animal passion. It wasn't an Olympic feat of uncontrolled lust but it just happened very gently and lovingly and as their rhythm increased slowly he never took his eyes from hers and when finally he came inside her, their release was total.

Both were carried to the heights of ecstasy, to the point of surrender, by pure emotion. Fulfilment was achieved through desire, through love, without the harshness of physical stimulation. Michael had no need to exercise control, she had no need of even his body. Their eyes, their voices, their feelings were enough. His attention never strayed from her and he was staring into her wide eyes and for a moment thought he would die from the pure pleasure of it all.

When they came it was together. For him it felt as if it would never stop, as if he would never empty, pulse-like he felt it pumping into her. For her she clung to him with all her strength, taking every drop of his sperm deep inside with pleasure and with joy.

For a long time they lay wrapped in each others arms. Without speaking and without guilt. Neither would allow sleep to disguise this moment. A calm perpetuity enshrouded them. One moment that they could extend by will.

Then much later as she lay warm and safe against him, her face resting softly on his chest, they started to talk again. She told him everything. About David's illness, her feelings, her confusion. He held her close and when she sobbed, he comforted her as if she were a child, running his fingers through her hair and stroking her face.

Although they knew that they should be together and were both absolutely certain of their feelings for each other, they also knew it couldn't be. The sadness that brought made them both silent, knowing that they must take and store the memories of this time but could not plan or promise anything to each other. Certainly they shared a hope that one day, somehow, they would be together and that it would be forever. But they also knew they faced many days of emptiness and nights of loneliness when they would act out a ritual with their partners and live with their feelings for each other locked deep within their minds. When they dressed it was again in silence and when he left and the door closed behind him they both felt an enormous weight descend and despair closed in upon them.

STILLBORN

CHAPTER SIX

As the months passed and winter turned to spring, David's work progressed. The necessary research was just about complete and he knew that he had seen his last winter as David Hawkin.

It had been a bad one, the words that transcended his thoughts were the title of Steinbeck's novel, 'The winter of our discontent'. Not only had he seen his own life petering out but many of his dreams had collapsed as well.

The physical deterioration had continued, he had lost a lot of weight and the skin was drawn across his skull like dried parchment. He slept little, lucky to snatch a few hours before the pain dragged him from sleep into the daily battle. He hadn't touched morphine yet, God knew he needed to, but prevalent in his mind was the desire to complete his work and for that he needed clarity not a drug induced haze. If he lived long enough then he knew at some stage such a foggy oblivion would be welcomed but he sincerely hoped that he could survive without it until the moment he surrendered his life for the experiment.

His relationship with Judy had also deteriorated although he still had no idea why. It just seemed to have turned into a continual battle. She had put up an emotional barrier that he couldn't penetrate.

"For God's sake Judy, what's wrong?"

"Nothing David. I'm just tired."

"You're always tired. That's if you're here at all! Extra work! Classes! What's it all about?"

"You can talk! The world's leading authority on workaholism!"

"Come on, be fair. I haven't got long left and there's so much to do."

"That's it!" She screamed, more angry at herself than him. She knew that she was being vicious but couldn't stop herself. "Same old bloody story. Poor David's dying! Nobody else is allowed to have a life."

He caught hold of her arms to try and reason with her but she broke away, turning so that she didn't have to look into that wretched face.

"I have needs too!"

"Yes! But you have a lifetime ahead of you," he collapsed onto a couch and allowed his head to drop onto his hands. He could hear Judy sobbing quietly and his anger soon dissipated and was replaced by guilt. Standing, he slowly walked up to her and gently put his arms around her, pulling her close to him. He felt her shudder as he touched her but attributed it to her anger. As always in these arguments logic played no part, the course they followed had become disturbingly routine. He knew he was right but always ended up feeling like a monster.

"I'm sorry darling," he said softly, nuzzling his face against the back of her neck and gently kissing that sensitive patch. And she felt just as guilty. She knew she was being awful to him. She was avoiding him, she hated him touching her and somehow it always ended up like this. First the argument, her self defence mechanism for trying to avoid sleeping with him. She hated doing it to him but couldn't help herself. Then, as always, she would end up in tears and he would be so submissive with that hurt look in his eyes. Then finally she would give in, her conscience dictating her actions. She turned and pulled his bowed head against her chest like a mother comforting a child she had scolded.

"I'm sorry David. I know I'm selfish. Its...its just my way of coping with things."

"Its alright Judy. I do understand."

But he didn't. He had no idea of what was going on in her mind. Every time he approached her she would pull away and then he would become angry. Deep down inside he knew she was rejecting him but he thought it was because she was disturbed by what was happening to them, that he was dying and that soon she would be on her own. He also assumed that her reaction was partly because of his physical deterioration, he knew he wasn't the most attractive of men in normal circumstances and now he was just skin and bone.

Then she would cry and he would add guilt to his low self-esteem and feel completely wretched and as an aftermath to their rows he would try and comfort her and hold her to him while she sobbed.

Eventually, having surrendered once again she would allow him to take her to bed and she would lie silently while he touched her until the nakedness of their bodies aroused him and he would begin to make love to her. But even as he did so he knew that he was using her and he didn't understand why this should be. He had a vague feeling of self disgust but by then it didn't matter. It was as if desire overrode his sensitivity. Their love making, if you could still call it that, did have one other beneficial side-effect. It helped him sleep. After orgasm, if he was lucky, he would drift off immediately. Without sex he sometimes lay there for most of the night, frustration combining with pain to fuel his insomnia.

This time, as usual, he led her to the bedroom. As

they undressed quietly there was no vestige of the feelings they had shared that first time they had been together six months earlier. She lay down next to him and pulled him close to her, preparing to submit to him again. His face was buried against her neck and she could feel his body close to her. She stiffened as she felt his habitual arousal and his lips opening against her skin. She surrendered as he started to move against her, preparing herself to submit but hating herself for doing so. He started moving down her body, his mouth seeking out her breasts. Instinctively, protectively, she held his head in her hands to stop him, she didn't want his lips on her breasts, no drawn out foreplay, she just wanted it over and done with.

"No not tonight, they feel funny."

"But..."

"No just put it in me David. Let me turn round, its nice that way." She wriggled round so that her back was towards him and pushed her bottom against him feeling his hardening penis touch her. One of his hands came around her and played with her breasts while he slid the other between her legs, searching out her clitoris.

"Arghhh" she feigned as his finger slid inside her. She didn't close her eyes and think of Michael but stared straight ahead, detaching herself from what was happening as she allowed him to use her body. Then he was inside her moving excitedly and she rocked her hips in rhythm.

"Oh that's so good. Faster! Come on faster!" She encouraged.

Her eyes closed and as she waited for him to satisfy himself she allowed her body to follow his demands while she focused her mind on other things. Funny, she thought, David was so thin and short but his penis was much larger than Michael's. It stopped there though, the difference was incredible. This was awful, she was being used by David while with Michael it was so different. She squeezed her buttocks trying to bring on his climax, her left hand went around him and she scratched the skin on his thigh with her nails.

"Faster! Come on. Yes. Yes!"

"Arghhhhh...."

She felt the wetness and was silent as he crushed himself against her. They said nothing to each other as he held her close. She could feel him becoming limp and waited for him to withdraw.

"Turn round David, let me cuddle you."

Sleepiily, he did as she said and turned over. She put an arm round him but instead of holding him close turned on her face so that they only touched lightly. He could feel drowsiness and a sense of guilt and loss. But the post coital effect allied to his weakened physical condition overcame those subtle feelings of self disgust and he quickly succumbed to the escape of sleep. Judy knew when he was asleep and carefully pulled her hand away, turning her back on him. She hugged the pillow and felt tears coming from her eyes. She tried to suppress her sobs so as not to disturb him and tried hard to picture Michael's face. For a long time she lay huddled like that, racked with guilt and sorrow, like a little girl who has been sent to bed early after having misbehaved. But like so many women who repeatedly allowed themselves to be used in this way, she felt despair and self hatred at what she had just done and what she knew she

would continue to do. Quietly she sobbed his name.
"Michael. Oh Michael."

Judy had found the last two months extremely difficult. Her feelings for Michael hadn't diminished at
all but had grown day by day. She found herself
thinking more and more of him and less of David.
Indeed the feelings she had retained for David were
now turning from apathy towards hate, she was
beginning to despise him almost as much as she hated
the predicament she was in.
When she and Michael became lovers they were
racked with guilt, she as David's fiancee, he as
David's best friend and Hannah's husband. Even so
in normal circumstances they would probably have
dealt with it, told the truth and picked up the pieces
of their lives.
What prevented this was David's illness. It was the
icing on the cake as far as their accumulated guilt
was concerned and it forced them to postpone the truth
until after his death. Judy hated herself for allowing
the charade to continue but was ashamed of the way
in which she was treating David. She also felt guilty
because although she loved Michael she knew that
she acted like a whore when she allowed David to
have sex with her.
She was certainly not equipped for the intrigue in
which she now found herself involved. Her upbringing had been strict if not severe. Her Catholic beliefs
and education gave her ingrained moral values that
now she was being forced to ignore. She hadn't been
to church let alone to confession since her
relationship with Michael had begun. Shame not
fear, kept her away.

STILLBORN

She had continued this anxious existence for several weeks before the real bombshell had dropped and it wasn't just the shock of what was happening, but the additional complications that she could have done without. When the realisation hit her it brought with it even more problems and at a time when she was finding everything difficult enough to cope with.

She had intuitively felt that something was wrong for a few days but without really analysing the cause or considering its implications. It was when, on the third morning in succession that the feeling of nausea rose within her that she finally came to terms with what was happening. After having been violently sick for no apparent reason, she was standing at the basin washing her face. Looking into the mirror she took note of her own reflection. She appeared changed somehow and it was at that instant that it came to her.

She was pregnant!

Panic gripped her. Not the warm feeling of motherhood and pride that should accompany the awareness of her condition, but blind panic.

'Whose was it?' Her reflection screamed at her in silent reproach.

She hurriedly dried herself. Fighting to regain composure she made her way back to the lab where she was working.

It was hopeless. As she stared into the screen of her computer terminal she was oblivious to the words displayed there. Beneath the glowing characters she could only see a reflection of her own anxious face. In despair she gave in to her panic. She picked up the phone and called Michael.

"Are you alone?"

"Yes, David's up with Jonas. What's wrong?"

"I've got to see you Michael," tears ran down her cheek and she touched the receiver with her fingers as if touching his face.

"Something terrible has happened."

"Okay Judy. Go home. I'll be right over."

Immediately she felt better knowing she would see him and that he would sort it out for her. She took a deep breath and composed herself at the same time wiping the tears from her cheeks. She called her supervisor and made an excuse that she didn't feel very well. Quickly she made her way out of the building and down the street to the underground.

Everything seemed unreal. She saw the blurred faces of other travellers as she made her way home. Some who she knew even spoke to her but she was deaf to their words. Absorbed with her own distress it seemed as if everybody knew. Every face seemed to look at her with censure, their eyes and unspoken words full of accusation. She struggled to keep control, focusing on an image of Michael, ignoring the thoughts and fears that threatened to overwhelm her. It only took ten minutes to get back to her apartment but to Judy it seemed like hours. Anxiously she placed her key in the lock and turned it before she stepped through the door. As it closed she breathed a momentary sigh of relief. Leaning against the wall she started to cry. Then she waited. Each minute seemed an eternity. She didn't move, just stayed where she was leaning against the wall for support, waiting for him to arrive.

Finally the door opened and she fell in to his arms, clutching him to her, a floodgate of tears suddenly released.

STILLBORN

"Hey. What is it?" He pulled her close holding her head against his broad shoulder and gently stroking her hair.

At first she couldn't tell him. She was afraid of his reaction but as he held her to him and she began to feel safe her sobs subsided and she managed to blurt out.

"Michael. I'm......I'm pregnant."

He sat with her and listened to all she had to say, letting it spill out amidst the tears. Not once did he interrupt her even after everything had been said and the torrent of words had ended in a trail of sobs. He just held her close, soothing her with his fingers in her hair, the warmth and strength of his body close to hers.

Later when she had stopped sobbing and lay quietly exhausted in his arms, he started to formulate a plan in his mind. He did not immediately share it with her, that was not his way of doing things. Michael relied to a great extent in both his work and for the way in which he conducted his personal life on his two greatest assets, his calm, controlled manner and a superb analytical approach to problem solving. Although his calmness was basically a natural characteristic of his personality, it had been developed even further during that part of his life, when as an athlete, he had excelled, and as a captain, he had needed to control both his, and his fellow team members' passions.

As he spoke to her in his gentle voice she looked at him, searching his eyes for a trace of the disgust she felt for herself. But there was no accusation. If anything a gentle smile seemed to mock her panic.

"Judy...you will have to take things one at a time.

108

First a pregnancy test, then your doctor should know," he stopped and turned to look out of the window. "I s'pose David will have to be told as well."

"I can't. Apart from anything else I don't know whose baby it is," she looked at him questioningly and was reassured as he pulled her closer to him.

"Look, what's happened is done now. Obviously I hope that you are carrying our child, but if it is David's... "

"What can I tell the doctor? I can't tell them you're the father and even if it is David's....."

"So don't tell them anything for now. You don't have to."

"But what if David finds out? I can't tell him about us and there's Hannah as well. So many people will be affected. Oh darling I don't care for myself but what about them and you...and..the baby?"

"Yes...the baby," he walked over to where Judy was sitting and placing his hands on her shoulders bent over and kissed her gently on the neck. "...you will have to tell them that David is the father. He won't deny it."

"But what about us?"

"Don't worry. I'll take care of that. I promise we will be together."

"But Hannah, I..?"

"Shhh, I said I'd take care of it."

"Oh Michael....will we really be together?"

"Yes, I promise," he leant over her and gazed into her lovely eyes, now warm and trusting.

"I promise."

STILLBORN

CHAPTER SEVEN

Spring gave way to summer and in turn the summer to the reds and golds of autumn.

As the leaves died and fell from the trees so David's life entered its final phase.

During the last few weeks, as they had reached the end of their preparation for the transfer of his spirit into a new life form, David's disease ravaged body had begun to surrender its tenuous hold on life and he had found it more and more difficult to keep himself motivated and resist the use of morphine with which to douse the pain that seared his back and internal organs.

The physical pain wasn't the only obstacle. Probably even more devastatating to David was the effects that the disintegration of his relationship with Judy were having. The combination of the disease and his own mental turmoil meant that his effectiveness in the laboratory had declined. Even so the work had progressed satisfactorily to the point that David felt they were ready to go ahead.

As always in nature, the old gives way to the young As one life form dies, another is born. So it was for David and the child that Judy was soon to bear, for as he came closer to death, so she came nearer to that point when she would bear his child.

Or so David believed.

The masquerade had been played well although with little relish on the part of its players, Judy and Michael. Torn as they were between their desires and their loyalties, they suffered more and more as each day passed. Their only consolation was the fact that the days were running out, soon they would be free of David and their guilt.

Jonas too had been busy with his own preparations and in keeping at bay the board members who once more pressed for cuts in expenditure. The recession was deepening and their cries were becoming shriller and more vindictive. But Jonas was a match for them, his cunning surpassed theirs, his greed was even greater and motivated him to go to any lengths to protect what he believed was his destiny. He knew that he hadn't long to wait, he could see the preparations were nearly complete, watched carefully at the way David was failing. His concern could be observed in the way he pushed David to go ahead as soon as was possible.

There was just one task left and it was a problem that David now addressed. The choice of his new parents, of the foetus whose body he would occupy. David's reaction to the print-out in front of him was initially one of disbelief. He just sat and stared at the words in front of him and couldn't believe what he saw there in black and white. He must be hallucinating. The doctor had warned him that the drugs did have side effects and the longer he took them the more the residual build up that could cause something like this. He shook his head, blinked rapidly and rubbed his eyes with his knuckles.
As his incredulity passed, the data that had shaken him so badly finally sunk in to the forefront of his mind.
Surprise gave way to consideration and the more he thought about it the more sensible it seemed.

STILLBORN

"No!" He cursed, screwing up the piece of paper and throwing it into the bin beside the desk. "Judy wouldn't go along with it and anyway, what of us, of Judy and I?"

He looked at the screen and quickly typed in a request.

Several other names scrolled the screen. David was looking but not seeing, while his fingers went through the processes, his mind was still considering what at first had seemed a ridiculous idea.

Suddenly he stopped and stared at the screen then slowly his gaze traversed across and down to the waste paper basket. He stared at it in a daze, slowly reached down and pulled out the crumpled piece of paper. He unfolded it then smoothed it out in front of him.

A glimmer appeared behind his tired eyes.

"Why not?" He asked himself. "Why not transfer into my own child?"

He paused in thought for several moments, chewing the end of the pencil he had been making notes with. Suddenly he snatched up the phone and called Judy. There was a moment's pause before her sleepy voice answered.

"Hi, Judy here."

"Judy I need to see you." "

Oh it's you David. What do you want? It's so late and I was in bed, I was just getting off to sleep," she yawned. "This had better be good."

"Oh it is Judy! This is better than good, its brilliant!"

Judy was suddenly more alert, there was something in David's voice that roused her, an excitement she hadn't heard for a long time. She glanced at the clock beside her bed and saw that it was nearly midnight.

It might be important to him, she thought, but it's so late. It can wait until morning.

"Can't it wait until morning? We can have breakfast together and talk about it then."

"No Judy. I'll be over in ten minutes."

"But..."

"Ten minutes Judy!" He shouted before slamming down the phone.

In fact it took him almost fifteen and by the time he arrived his agitation had only increased. Although he was making every effort he could not calm himself, there were just too many things to say, too much in his head that he wanted to share with Judy.

Even before the door had closed behind him he took hold of her arm and pulled her round to face him.

"Judy?"

She was startled. His call and his insistence at coming over had annoyed her. Now she was worried and a little frightened at what David was going to say and do next.

"What is it David? What is so important that it can't wait until morning, that you had to drag me out of bed to tell me?"

"The baby Judy.....I ran a compatibility program to start selecting the foetal recipient for my transfer. Guess who the computer came up with?"

"Who?" She asked in a trembling voice. The expression on her face, the way her eyes were beginning to widen said that she already knew the answer.

"You...us...our baby! Well? What do you think?"

"Oh my God! You can't be serious?"

The smile slipped from his face. He looked at her with growing uncertainty, the expression on her face. What was it she was feeling? Anger? Disgust?

113

STILLBORN

Hatred? In an instant all the emotions she had suppressed for nine months welled up inside her, threatening to burst out.

"For God's sake David...you can't mean it?"

The colour drained from her face and she seemed to gulp in air.

"Why not?" He asked her. "Its perfect! The genetic make-up would be the closest possible outside of a clone!"

Judy was on the point of hysteria and didn't know what to do. She wanted to scream at him, beat him with her fists, smash that sycophantic face of his. Inside she was demented, on the point of collapse or explosion, either could happen.

Neither did.

Instead she sucked in a deep breath and looked him dispassionately in the eyes.

"Wait! Just hold it David, I have to think," then she turned and strode into her bedroom and slammed the door shut behind her.

David felt as if he had been left in a vacuum. He looked around with a puzzled expression on his face then sank down into a chair and tried to think, sort out in his mind just what had happened, what was going on. Judy was upset. Fine. What else could he expect, it was a shock, it had taken him aback, taken him a while to get used to the idea. She needed time to think as well.

Then just as suddenly as the idea had made his spirits soar so they fell as he considered all the other implications. If he became his own father? He asked himself, how could his own son form a relationship with Judy? And that had been one of the main reasons why he had decided to proceed as the guinea

114

pig. To have the chance of being reunited with Judy. In the moments that passed, while he sat there deep in thought, successive ideas struck home. Firstly, the relationship with Judy had not proceeded as well as he had at first imagined it would. Secondly, could he reasonably expect her to want him when he was someone else. The thought at first depressed him but even as he felt despair creep over him he realised that he too would be another person, perhaps with different likes and dislikes. Perhaps he would not want to be with her either. Certainly, he thought, I love Judy. But in what way? Its not entirely physical, more a meeting of minds, a convergence of ideas. He was not even certain of which aspects of his being he would retain when born again. Was love transferable? He asked himself. He had no answer.

So the problem and the solutions continued to evolve within his mind. With the facts and the dredged up emotions, he threw in his current desires. As death approached these had changed. His physical weakness had eroded his sexual needs, increased his desire for love and compassion. He came to the conclusion that when reborn she would be his mother and perhaps that would be just as rewarding as her being his lover.

With this acceptance a new excitement rose within him. He felt certain that this would be the correct path to take. The spirit from his dying body would be transferred into the body of his unborn son.

"Judy!" He yelled, making his way towards the bedroom. "Judy!"

All pain and self pity were temporarily forgotten, lost in the excitement of this concept, subdued by this moment of euphoria.

STILLBORN

"Judy, its alright. It will be alright!"

"I'm just coming David."

She splashed some cold water on her face and quickly dried herself. Then standing upright and with an inward shrug and a toss of her head, she turned towards the door ready to face David once more.

"But Michael! He wants me to be the recipient. He wants to use me in his damned experiment. How can you take it all so calmly? That may be our child growing inside me. Do you want David crawling around inside our child's head? Its not natural! Christ, you can't agree to that!"

"I said don't worry and I meant it. I'll take care of everything, David won't be controlling the experiment, I will."

"What can you do? You can't interfere. Jonas will be there. The whole thing will be recorded. Its horrible!"

Michael pulled her towards him and held her head against his chest, gently letting his hands run through her hair.

"I said it will be alright, didn't I? Don't you trust me?"

"I don't know," she answered desperately.

Michael pulled her chin towards him so that he looked into her mournful eyes, his own laughing back at her in mock reproach. She felt the warmth rise inside her, felt his body close to hers. Strong, hard muscled and yet so gentle.

"Yes, Michael, you know I do."

"Well then?"

"But how can you stop it?"

"By making sure his spirit escapes." He paused and

116

stroked the hair back off her forehead.

"Its quite easy really," his soft voice was so soothing she closed her eyes.

"In every experiment so far, if there is a way out the spirit escapes. It doesn't seem to matter whether there is a recipient or not. Somehow the selection is already made and wherever possible the spirit will make its way to its predestined goal. If you think about it, the chances are that you aren't the one that is chosen to receive David's spirit. That would be a one in a million chance. So all I have to do is to arrange a way out. Its as simple as that."

"But what about David, he...he'll die."

"No he won't, his spirit will pass on to where it should have gone." He leant over and brushed her eyelids with his lips.

"Yes. I see." She opened her eyes and looked up into his smiling face.

"One day he'll be able to tell the whole world. Shouldn't think for a minute anyone will believe him though," he laughed as a picture swum before his eyes. "Especially if he is reincarnated as the child of a call-girl in Soho..., or...ha..ha...a Russian KGB officer, you know Eva someone, like that bag in James Bond with knives coming out of her boots....or perhaps..."

"A lesbian! An artificially inseminated lesbian!" She joined in.

"Or aaah..ha-ha a fucking ladybird! Ah ha ha ha," he whooped with laughter and so did she.

For minutes they couldn't speak as they laughed at the different pictures they created of David's would be mother.

It was good to see her laugh, thought Michael, it had

been a while. He pulled her close and as the laughter subsided she looked at him seriously, was about to ask a question. He placed a finger on her lips to stop her.

"Anyway, even if he turns out to be our next door neighbour or the prime minister...it won't be for a long, long time," he chuckled as he pulled her close to him. He was more serious now but tried to keep a little light-heartedness in his voice.

"I like David but I don't want his clone knocking on our door and trying to date our daughter!"

Immediately she succumbed, both mentally and physically. She had complete confidence in him and knew that he would protect them both from whatever came along.

"You are clever Michael, and so sensible. Do you know something, I really have come to rely on you. Before we became lovers I used to feel so much in control of myself. But that's all changed now. It feels so good having someone to trust, to share things with."

She lifted her head and kissed him gently under his chin, her fingers running lightly across his strong chest.

"I love you so much Michael."

He kissed her gently and smiled.

She closed her eyes, feeling at peace again. For the moment she was with him and all her troubles were miles away. She felt safe in Michael's arms.

The smile on his face hid darker thoughts. In his mind he rehearsed once again his own plans.

David's spirit wouldn't die. He couldn't carry that responsibility. But he would make sure that he couldn't come back to haunt them.

118

CHAPTER EIGHT

The night lights in the laboratory cast their orange glow over the two men who were still working. The subdued atmosphere was only interrupted by the flashing of console indicators and the background hum of machinery, as the vast array of equipment continued its handling of data, undeterred by the fact that it was nearly four in the morning.

A weary and haggard looking man stretched and took a deep breath at the same time rubbing sleep from his eyes with his knuckles.

"Its done."

Michael who was poring over some figures, stopped what he was doing and turned slowly to look at the speaker.

"Everything is ready. We can start the experiment at any time."

As David spoke he wondered at his own emotions. It all seemed such an anti climax and the overwhelming feeling of tiredness seemed to drown any feelings of elation that he, as a scientist, should expect to feel at this moment in time. He was at the threshold of his greatest achievement and it seemed to mean so little to him. Perhaps that was not so unreasonable, considering what he now had to go through.

He stretched and yawned, his scrawny arms pointing towards the ceiling like sticks. The yawn turned into a cough and that became a spasm that shook his fragile body. He grabbed the inhaler and squirted the tranquilliser into his protesting lungs, the cough turned into a rapid panting. Then he slowly calmed down.

STILLBORN

Michael watched him and felt something akin to revulsion tinged with guilt. It was as if he himself had brought this upon David. Little of the old friendship remained, David's innocent possession of Judy for all these months had caused Michael's feelings to swing through the spectrum from love to a sort of apathy.

The indulgent smile on his face hid his feelings well. As David turned back to face Michael there were tears in his eyes brought there by the searing pain. He was feeling the effects of the tremendous effort they had sustained in reaching this point, working every day of the week and often late into the night. At the same time he had somehow managed to withstand the disease that grew in his body while refusing most of the time to take any medication to relieve the pain. Then there were the other problems that hung like a leaden weight on his soul. The future had changed so devastatingly, just nine months ago he was happy and secure in his work and engaged to marry a wonderful girl whom he loved very much. Now there was to be no marriage and he was about to die, his relationship with Judy had just about fallen apart. She was about to have their child and he would never see it. At least not as a father and husband would.

Even in the few days he had left there was little to enjoy. The relationship with Judy had gone sour. He had made so many excuses for the changes in her but in his mind he knew it had just gone wrong. The most frustrating thing was that he didn't really know why. He just hoped that she would be a better mother than a wife.

As Michael spoke he sighed inwardly and tried to push away such self destructive thoughts.

"So when do we begin?"

"Tomorrow, day after. Judy is in her final week of the pregnancy already, if we delay things much longer we will have to keep her out of labour," he yawned. "I think the best thing we can do now is to go home. We could both use some sleep and later tomorrow I'll see Jonas and obtain his final sanction. After that, well...that's it, bit of an anti climax really, isn't it?."

"No! Wait until tomorrow, you'll feel better. Surely you could take a bit more time for yourself, after all..."

"I can't Michael, I just haven't got that much time left and if I'm really honest, I don't think I want that much longer. It hasn't been easy living like this you know."

Michael glanced at David and felt the weight of sorrow and guilt bear down on him. The situation with Judy was almost unbearable. He longed to be with her and felt an aching hunger when he didn't see her. Yet even with such strong feelings of love for her he felt like a thief because Judy had belonged to this man, and David had also been very dear to him at one time. He took a deep breath and swallowed in an effort to drown his guilt. When he spoke it was without looking directly into David's eyes.

"Are you staying here tonight?"

"No. I'm going home. There are a few things I have to sort out in the morning, have to arrange for the flat to be cleared, give the keys to the landlord. Just a few odds and ends." Michael stifled a sigh of relief.

"You get off home then. I'll close down. Get a good night's rest and don't rush things tomorrow, I'll look after everything."

121

STILLBORN

"Thanks Michael. I really don't know what I would have done without you." He smiled gratefully and noticed again how Michael quickly averted his eyes. I suppose it's difficult for him too, he thought. I look such a mess and he just doesn't want me to see the pity in his eyes.

"I'll call a cab for you."

"OK. See you tomorrow Michael."

The support that Michael had lent him over the last few months had been incredible. He had taken on so much of the work load and David knew that without him they would never have completed everything in time.

He got up with an obvious effort and started to make his way to the door, his mind still on his friend. It was strange, he thought, that while Michael had been so supportive at work they had seemed to have so little contact outside working hours. Still, he decided, that was probably because they were both so tired and his friend had obvious difficulty in coming to terms with David's condition. During the past nine months, almost since Judy became pregnant, he seemed to have changed in his attitude towards David. Thinking back, he could remember when he first noticed the changes. It was after the last time they had spent an evening together, the four of them, at that French restaurant.

Then there was Judy. Their relationship had altered so much and David longed for that closeness of their first few days of really being together. That too had changed and he felt as if Judy had really distanced herself from him. Although he had tried to tell her of his feelings, she always seemed to avoid the subject so that he would be left with an empty feeling and a sour taste in his mouth. With a sigh he closed the door behind him and made his way slowly to the street to wait for his cab.

For a split second David gazed at these coincidences as they drifted through his mind. He almost made the connection. Perhaps he even considered the possibility of Judy and Michael. If he did, it was at a level that was quickly dismissed by his conscious mind.

It was a clear night. The deserted pavements were still damp from the earlier rain and the lights of the city twinkled in the pre-dawn. David took a deep breath, it tasted good. It was the time of day when pollution was at its lowest, traffic having all but ceased some hours earlier. Still the city smells persisted but they were something David was used to, even fond of. They reminded him of the many cultures and nationalities that shared life in this metropolis. London, these days, carried the scents of the Arab souk, Portuguese fishing ports, African villages, New York, Paris.

God he'd miss all this!

He turned as his cab approached and watched it as it glided to a stop beside him. He leaned in through the passenger window.

"You've come for me? David Hawkin?"

"Yes Guv. Jump in."

David opened the back door and getting in, settled himself in the seat.

"Where to?"

"Oh..53 Edith Road, West Ken."

"Right you are."

He had told Michael he was going home because it was so late and he didn't want to disturb Judy. He had also said that there were some loose ends he wanted to tidy up in the morning. All of this was true but it wasn't the whole truth. He wanted to be on his own. The time had arrived. He needed what little was left to be spent in solitude so that he could be clear about his plans and how he would accomplish what he had set his mind on.

As the cab moved off he clutched his briefcase on his knees and let his mind wander again. She probably finds it difficult too, difficult to be close to someone who won't be there for much longer.

Then there was the baby.

The cab moved on its solitary journey west along the embankment. David glanced out and watched a barge edging its way slowly up the south bank. There was a man in a donkey jacket on deck, happily puffing a pipe as he manoeuvred the heavily laden craft. David looked but didn't see. The city was empty and reflected his mood, his desolate feeling of being cut off from the world.

Damn!, he thought, I feel so alone.

The cab took the 'tourist's' route' turning north at Victoria then around Hyde Park corner and down Knightsbridge. David wouldn't have noticed if they had travelled via Luton. Minutes later they pulled up in the middle of the road outside his flat.

"Six pounds fifty guv."

David absently passed the man a crumpled ten pound note rescued from some recess of his coat pocket. He didn't even glance at it to ascertain its value.

He stepped out of the cab and wandered to his door ignoring the driver's vague efforts at offering him his change. He put his key in the lock and turned.

"Right, thanks guv. Have a good night...er..mornin"

"Night."

Inside his bedroom he undressed lackadaisically, allowing his clothes to stay where they fell.

He stepped into the bathroom and gazed without recognition at the emaciated face in the mirror.

He didn't bother to wash or clean his teeth but he did take some medication, a large dose.

It was over, his work was done.

It didn't matter now.

For a change he got straight into bed. He didn't read or even spend any time mulling over the day's events as he would have done before the illness.

Exhausted, he closed his eyes and surrendered almost instantly to his tiredness, falling quickly into a drugged and dreamless sleep.

Occasionally as he slept his body would flinch and his lips would draw back as he winced with pain.

In the few moments it had taken for David to travel home, Michael had tidied up the laboratory and checked that everything was in place for the next day. Closing the laboratory door he hadn't made his way to the stairs and out of the building. Instead he had left the room by the back door which now led into the small flat in which Judy had been living for the last few weeks. David had insisted on this; the rooms were lined with the lead alloy that protected Judy's foetus from the intrusion of any other wandering soul. She was also close by in case there were any other complications. If she did go into labour they could control things with drugs. If David suddenly became worse and was dying, the transfer could take place. Judy had objected but in this case David was insistent and was able to rely on good scientific common sense in order to persuade her.

STILLBORN

Michael walked silently through the combined living room cum kitchen and into her bedroom. He stopped and listened, allowing time for his senses to adjust. It was silent apart from her breathing and the steady drone of the air conditioning. The room was entirely lined, there were no external windows. The only light in the room was from the small indicators on the console close to the bed. It wasn't much but soon it was enough for Michael to see her outline, then her features. She lay on her side, knees drawn up, hands on top of each other beneath her left cheek. Her mouth was slightly apart, full lips pouting childishly in sleep. Her hair lay tousled around her head and on her pillow, dark and silken it reflected the little amount of light in the room.

Michael walked over silently and bent over her. Very softly he pressed his lips to hers, kissing her gently. She sighed and a small smile lit her sleeping face.

He saw her lips mouth 'I love you too'.

Michael left as quietly as he came.

CHAPTER NINE

All in all it had been a good pregnancy. The morning sickness had abated after only a couple of weeks and since then she had really suffered very little discomfort although the rapidly changing state of her body took its toll and she tired easily and would sometimes sleep for twelve hours at a stretch. Since the baby had started moving, Judy had given her situation a lot more thought. It was strange that according to what Michael had told her, that wriggling baby inside her was still nobody, had no soul, was an empty vessel waiting to be filled. It made her feel warm and protective but at the same time her feelings were very confused. Her natural abhorrence at the idea of producing a reincarnated David was totally at odds with the strong maternal feelings that had developed along with her pregnancy. She tried very hard to blot out that part, to deny what David wanted to happen to her. She prayed that Michael's plans would ensure that David's spirit would not be planted in the tiny body of her unborn child.

Of course there was another aspect to consider, who was her baby's biological father? The truth was she had no idea but if hope and love were of any value it must certainly be Michael's. Funny, she thought, this extra element in heritage would become quite a subject if David's program was successful. Previously there was only one uncertainty that parents had to consider. Who was the biological father of a child? It may be that in years to come, people would want to know who was the spiritual parent of their baby? The natural progression would be to choose a spirit for

127

your child to be. Almost certainly it would become the basis of a whole new industry.

'Choose a spirit. Register with GENE-IS-IS, the premier spiritual introduction agency. Thousands of souls to choose from. Allow our computers to introduce you to dying people whose souls may include just the one you want for your baby. Hurry while stocks last. All fees fully refundable if you don't get the soul you are looking for. This month's special - ex university professor and amateur tennis champion....only £10,000.'

She laughed at the comedy in such a possibility but inwardly there was perhaps a grimace at the probability of such a scene. Only man as he continually interfered with nature was capable of such a perversion.

As she showered on this particular morning, she was surprised that she had a wonderful sense of well being. Coming out of the cubicle she stood naked in front of the full size mirror and looked at her reflection. Her eyes were focused on her tummy but her peripheral vision took in the overall shape of her naked body. Although her figure was now considerably distorted, she took pleasure in what she saw and smiled to herself. There was perhaps an added beauty that she was surprised to see. Her pregnancy looked somehow right, carried as it was on her athletic frame. Her long legs and tanned skin somehow seemed even healthier and more alive than usual. Her hands caressed her tummy lovingly and she allowed herself a moment to imagine her baby as a small boy, a man. An image seemed to rest there in her mind, a mental overlay was formed and she could almost see her baby curled in its foetal position within her stomach. Its very fragility and dependence endeared it to her.

Then in her day-dream she imagined she saw it move. Its head, much too large for its tiny body, turned to face her in the mirror image that her mind played tricks with. She smiled and focused on the eyes that stared at her and seemed to grow as if rushing towards her. Suddenly she held her breath, recognition startling her. The eyes were not a baby's eyes. She knew those eyes and as they came closer and grew even bigger she saw they were David's eyes, pain filled and haunted. The face too was his. Old and wizened, drawn and skull like. He stared at her with an expression of hate, this monster that her mind had created. She could feel the enmity burn into her, saw his mouth break open in a toothless grimace of accusation.

Judy screamed and the sound of her voice filled her ears. She closed her eyes and blotted out the vision.

Jonas was listening with half his mind as David went over the preparations for the final stages of the program that would see the end of David Hawkin and the beginning of much greater things for all those involved. Meanwhile he concentrated his mind on how he would accomplish his primary objective, which was to come out of this with a seat on the board. During the past six months he had thought of little else and fortunately there had been no other major issues that would have taken up too much of his time at work. He was sitting back in the soft cushions of his chair, his ample frame relaxed, huge fingers interlaced and resting on his belly. On his face he wore a benign, kindly expression. The kind of look that politicians reserved for mothers with children in their arms when the press were close at hand.

Jonas thought he knew exactly what lay in store for him and had come up with what he considered to be a foolproof plan. The fact that David was announcing a time and date brought the whole matter into vivid reality. Jonas was not immune to feelings of excitement, even trepidation.

Looking now at David's withered appearance he felt little sense of guilt over his intentions to steal the limelight from the dying man. After all, he told himself, it wasn't his fault that David was in his current predicament and he would allow the professor a fair proportion of the accolades, albeit posthumously. What really bothered him was the other one, David's assistant. He wouldn't feel any guilt over that man either. He was a foreigner, a social primitive. But he knew of Michael's background and knew of his resourcefulness and accepted that he was not an adversary to be dismissed lightly. Still, he decided, he's no match for Jonas Nichols.

Then he let his thoughts wander onwards to his future and how the outcome of the next few weeks would see the fulfilment of his ambitions. For surely, he thought, as well as the inevitable election to the board he would become a celebrity, achieve notoriety as the saviour of mankind. The gift he was bringing to the human race was a gift from the gods, eternal life.

Now his smile was even broader and lost in his own self indulgent thoughts he hadn't noticed that he was being asked a question.

"You will be there, won't you Jonas?"

"Ahem, what did you say?"

"I was just asking if you will be there tomorrow? Late morning?"

"Oh yes, I'll be there. Wouldn't miss it for the world." Then trying hard to erase his smile and put on a suitably austere expression he added somewhat belatedly. "And don't you worry about a thing. Don't forget you are not exactly leaving us, it won't be long and we will all be sitting around this desk again enjoying the rewards of your success. In the meantime I'll see that Judy is well looked after too."

"Thank you Jonas," David rose from his seat and started to leave the room.

"Don't you worry....and don't forget to tell that man of yours to come and see me. There are things I need to discuss with him."

Michael walked into the office and with some misgivings took the seat offered him by the head of their department. As he looked into the big man's eyes he felt a little uneasy. He knew that Jonas Nichols was a shrewd, perhaps even cunning man and he had recognised the power hungry glint in his eye more than once. He had remarked on it to David but his friend had dismissed this in his usual naive and preoccupied way. Luckily for him he also knew that Jonas was more of an administrator than a scientist although he obviously must have had a scientific background of some sort or other, long ago and long forgotten. Certainly when Jonas came to the laboratory he seemed oblivious to what was actually going on. If Michael was submitting a technical explanation he had noticed that opaque look in his eyes when the conversation became in any way complex. He had also noticed the way that Jonas seemed to hurry over such matters.

Today Jonas was full of smiles and courtesies. This wasn't the way he normally acted around his staff, particularly with Michael who had long been aware of a sense of animosity. He knew from past experience that the big man had little time for foreigners and had more than once felt his eyes upon him and on looking up was met with a slightly condescending look.

"Thank you. How can I help?"

"Let us get comfortable first. Would you like a drink? No. Ok, lets get on with business then. Look, I know you are fully aware of what David is about to undertake and that it has my approval, albeit unspoken. I can't be seen to approve of what he is about to do or I would be hauled up before the board and that would be the end of my career. The same goes for you, young man. So I thought it would be a good time to corroborate our stories so to speak."

"I wouldn't do anything behind his back."

"No.. Of course not. All I want to do is protect us all, the professor as well. No point in any of us getting into more trouble than necessary."

"Yes, that makes sense."

"I've prepared a document which Professor Hawkin has signed. It eliminates us from any responsibility over his actions. I thought it only fair to let you see it. Here you are, just take your time."

Michael took the document and read through carefully, discovering it to be exactly as the director had indicated. He quickly reappraised Jonas's motives, perhaps he wasn't so bad after all. Certainly he was protecting himself but he seemed to have extended that protection to Michael as well. The document clearly indicated that David's actions were his own and that neither Jonas or Michael were involved.

It was a suicide note.

"What about David, I mean Professor Hawkin? Surely this document will be very damaging for him?"

"I don't think so Michael. David accepts full responsibility for ending his own life but then he won't be here to answer any questions or be punished in any way, will he?"

"No. I suppose not."

"Of course not! Well not for a long time anyway and by the time he is back with us I am sure that the fuss will have been forgotten, especially in the light of the results. Wouldn't you agree?"

"Well, yes I suppose so." The frown on Michael's face relaxed and he smiled at Jonas. "Yes I agree.... but I wouldn't want him to suffer any more than he has to."

"I'm glad you brought the matter of his suffering up Michael. He has been looking very ill lately, I really don't know how he has carried on. Anyway! I don't think either of us would like to see him go through any more than he has to. I have a suggestion as to how we can help in that direction as well."

"Yes?"

"Well......letting the poor man administer the drug to himself that will kill him is a bit callous, isn't it?. So I've come up with a plan that will make it easier for him but I do need your help."

"I'll do anything I can to help David through this."

"Good, good. Now what I propose is this,"

STILLBORN

Jonas leant forward and spoke in a conspiratorial whisper. As Jonas explained what he wanted Michael to do, the American was at first shocked then the idea gradually seemed to make sense. Jonas went into more details of why he had decided to act in this way, that it was in David's best interests - Jonas was very persuasive.

"You make certain that everything is ready now. I'll give you an hour or so but call me straight away if there are any problems. Ok?"

"Yes...but.."

"I'll come down to the laboratory and we'll give David a bit of a send off. More than he will expect I think," he chuckled to himself but quickly caught Michael's shocked expression and turned the rising laughter into a coughing spasm. "I'll bring champagne but his will be drugged. He won't be expecting anything as we've already agreed. Tomorrow is the day, so his ahem... departure...should be swift and painless."

"But..."

"Now be a good chap and make sure everything is ready. Bring me some of whatever drug he was intending to use and make sure it's a big dose, don't want to mess this up do we?"

"Is all this necessary sir?" Michael interrupted, doubt filling his eyes. "It does change the whole ball game you know. Simple suicide is becoming murder."

"Bah! Nonsense young man. At worst we will be assisting him in what is voluntary euthanasia. Don't go all ethical on me now! Think of the professor.....this will be a much more satisfactory ending for him, don't you agree?"

"I suppose so. At least he won't know its coming until its too late."

"That's right. Anyway we've always got the suicide note, eh?.," Jonas clamped a huge hand on Michael's shoulder and started to chuckle. Suddenly he stopped laughing and looked at Michael quite seriously. "I must remind you, complete secrecy or we could be in hot water."

Michael thought about it for a moment, wondering if Jonas had any other motives. Jonas knew he was being scrutinised and did his best to appear impassive and relaxed. Finally Michael shrugged off the uneasy feeling he had. He couldn't see any reason not to go along with Jonas's scheme.

"Okay. I'll get the drugs from the dispensary. Everything will be ready in an hour."

Jonas had been holding in his breath, waiting to see if he had succeeded in persuading Michael to become his accomplice. He let it escape slowly, hiding the inward relief he felt behind a good humoured and impassive expression.

"Good, fine. Now obviously the safety of the experiment will be in your hands. You are the only person who understands fully what is involved. Are you completely confident?"

"You don't have to worry about that. David and I have covered every detail."

"Good. I am relying on you. I couldn't begin to understand all the technicalities involved. Not only is the reputation of the department at stake but Professor Hawkin's life will be literally, in your hands." He looked across at Michael with what was surely genuine concern showing in his eyes. Michael replied with a smile and a nod of his head.

"Now just one other matter. The Professor's departure will create a staff vacancy. I can't see any advantage in getting a stranger in to run the department so I would like you to take over, obviously on increased salary etc. Can I rely on your cooperation young man? Can you cope?"

That benevolent smile that politicians reserve for young mothers and babies was back on his face but Michael was so taken aback that he didn't see the sly glint in the director's eye. He had certainly misjudged the man, he thought. He really is quite considerate. The stories about his dislike of foreigners must be just gossip.

"You can rest assured that everything will run smoothly Jonas."

"Oh I'm sure it will."

CHAPTER TEN

The little group of people stood within the sealed chamber that had been constructed in the laboratory and raised their glasses.

Finally the moment had arrived, a moment built upon millions of years of human endeavour and ingenuity. Until now man's interference with nature had only scratched the surface, finally he hoped to transcend the barrier of death and in so doing perhaps discover the meaning of life itself.

"To David, to wish him well on his journey," Judy said softly. She put an arm around him and kissed his cheek. Her sombre eyes never quite met his.

David lifted his glass to acknowledge the toast. A smile flickered around his drawn mouth but his eyes remained dull.

David had suffered from very mixed feelings in the days preceding this one. The scientist had been looking forward eagerly to this moment, the man with his human fears was somewhat reluctant to actually bring about his own death. The lover was tired, wistfully hoping things were as they had been a year earlier, glad that he would be escaping the current nightmare their relationship had become.

Judy had gritted her teeth and held on. She resigned herself to endure whatever she had to during these last few weeks knowing that it would be over soon. At least she was able to avoid intercourse with David, the stage of her pregnancy was an acceptable excuse. Judy had been living in the small alloy lined flat at the CDG laboratories for three weeks and was relieved that soon she would escape that too. David had been adamant that she stay there and she had acceded much against her will. It was another step in the dissolution of their relationship but one which she was prepared to endure in the circumstances.

Part of the laboratory had been converted, providing her with a bedroom, shower room and living area. Her food was brought in from the canteen although there was a small refrigerator in the corner of the living room and she also had a kettle and toaster. It had been adequate rather than comfortable.

"Thank you Judy," he hung on to her a moment, his head buried in her long hair.

Michael had been very busy during those last few days and had spent most of his waking hours in the laboratory, checking every detail of the preparations for the transfer, hardly stopping to eat or rest. Apart from his duties which took up most of his time, he would also have been found in the lonely hours before dawn, furtively making alterations to the chamber in which they now stood. He was pleased with his own preparations and with the solution he had devised to protect Judy's unborn child from the intrusion of David's spirit.

He too comforted himself with the knowledge that it would all be over soon, that he and Judy would be together and he would be able to escape those unwanted dreams. He was becoming consumed by his feelings which were indeed diverse. Feelings of love, guilt and jealousy which hounded him throughout his days and nights. When he did finish working it was with great difficulty and finally with the aid of drugs that he would fall into a fitful sleep. Sleep that allowed no escape from his predicament, just a series of vivid nightmares filled with pictures of a naked Judy and a grotesque David who was making love to her. Sometimes she was being raped by David but in the worst of his nightmares she was willing and would be greedily satisfying herself on David's disgusting body. They would be clinging to each other, drenched with sweat. He would be trapped in his dream, watching, unable to stop them. Always the dream ended in the same way with Judy in the last throes of childbirth, her legs stretched wide apart and a small and wrinkled head being forced out of her vagina. The half born baby would turn and look at him and it was David's features that would break open in a toothless grin.

Michael would wake from these nightmares, cold and shaking, the seeming reality of these cruel enactments was difficult to shake off and it would be hours before he could sleep again.

Now it was all coming to an end. Finally Michael would be able to rid himself of his dreams and he and Judy would be able to plan a life together.

So it was with a sense of relief and growing anticipation that he too lifted his glass at Judy's direction. Although wishing David bon voyage, his own private toast was to Judy and himself and to their future together.

"Good luck David."

"Goodbye Michael," David put an arm around Michael and leant a tired head on his strong shoulder.

STILLBORN

Jonas had also been fully occupied recently. Many an hour he had spent poring over the notes and reports that David had prepared until he was fully aware of how the mechanics of the experiment were to be conducted. He found it difficult to grasp some of the more technical aspects of the processes involved but what he lacked in technical expertise, he more than made up for with practical ability and cunning. Then there was another matter to which he had given careful consideration, a puzzle, which in order to unravel he had devoted much of his resources and time. He had wanted to find out exactly what had been going on between Judy & Michael.

His suspicions arose when noticing the covert glances, the absences from work by the foreigner. Being a man who covered his options he had made it his business to get to the bottom of that particular mystery. Using departmental resources he hired a detective to find out and now he finally had the proof of their little 'menage a trois'. The evidence, the report and photographs, was tucked away in Jonas's safe for possible future use.

Finally the time had arrived when he was to put his plans in motion and he would be relieved when this day was over. Although on one hand he enjoyed the challenge and the intrigue, he also found that the mounting tension rising within him was creating an unwanted sense of nervousness, a feeling that he would be glad to escape.

The moment had arrived and the seconds seemed to stretch as he waited to see the others join the toast.

It was not without a megalomaniac's confidence and sense of self-righteousness that he awaited the product of his connivance.

140

Jonas lifted his glass to these inconsequential people and proposed his own toast and even savoured the taste of the wine as it reached his palate.

"To you David, a fruitful journey. I look forward to your return."
"Thank you Jonas".

Michael finally forced himself to look into David's eyes and raising his glass to his lips allowed the liquid to trickle down his throat.

"Thank you, all of you," said David and also drank.

As ill as he was, David still enjoyed the moment.
Then in that brief instant of pleasure came panic, fear borne of recognition occurring almost within the same instant that he swallowed.
Almost at once he became aware of the effects of the drug within the wine.
Already it was too late and it was with some surprise that David felt a dark curtain descend upon his vision and numbness course through his body.
He felt himself slide to the floor and weakly struggled to overcome the inevitable. His disease ravaged body was in no condition to mount a defence to the toxicity of the drug and as he slid down the irreversible slope towards oblivion he was only vaguely aware of the pinprick as a needle was inserted into the vein of his arm. The drug didn't kill instantly but the induced coma occurred within seconds and left him helplessly trapped within a paralysed body just waiting for death.
When finally his heart struck its final beat the

expected oblivion did not come. Like all before him he experienced the sudden clarity of those moments that closely preceded and even followed death. His lifetime's experiences flashed by compacted by the hormone induced hyperactivity of his brain. He experienced those brief moments when he felt his spirit rise from within his body and was able to look down on the lifeless form that was once his own.

Then unlike any man before him that awareness did not fade as the last vestiges of brain function no longer supported the mortal aspects of his consciousness. For David, his human integrity was maintained as his spirit began its transition to secure its place within a new life form.

It was with shock and surprise that Michael found he too had been poisoned.

He knew the drug, recognised instantly what had happened, guessed there had been a mistake with the glasses.

'Perhaps it was no mistake' his subconscious offered. The idea hit his mind like an explosion, galvanising him into action.

He was not weakened by disease, had a strong body and a very firm resolve. These strengths combined with his anger to mount a defence. Adrenaline coursed through his veins and built a temporary barrier to the inevitable effects of the drug. Fear and an unreconcilable sense of loss pervaded his being and he struggled desperately to focus his eyes, to locate the source of his fear and loss. Still swaying he watched his beloved Judy crumple and fall close to a couch and he staggered like a puppet on strings towards her, finally falling within an arms length.

He forced his eyes to turn and seeing her unconscious form was unable to comprehend why this was happening. Through sheer strength of will he made his arm move, reaching with enormous effort until his fingers touched hers and in that moment preceding paralysis he managed to utter his last words.

"I love you Judy".

He took a final gulp of air and controlled the flow of oxygen into his blood stream. His body had ceased to function but he had not yet surrendered consciousness.

Behind her he could see Jonas.

The big man stood poised over the inert form of David. Michael saw him plunge a syringe into David's right arm and saw the look of satisfaction form around the big man's mouth. He struggled to focus and before losing that fight it came to him clearly.

He understood what was happening. It was too late for him to act and he knew that it did not really matter now for he had started on a new journey and at least would share that path with Judy. For an instant he felt that he would succumb to panic as he struggled to close the spiritual gap between Judy and himself, to ensure that they would be together at least in death. There was a moment of uncertainty, he could not feel her presence only the closeness of another struggling spirit from which he tried to free himself. As his own consciousness slipped away he realised that the other spirit that was close to him belonged to David.

Jonas had little time to waste, he had practised the necessary actions over and over in his mind. The first thing he had to do was to administer the necessary injections to preserve the memory of the dying man, to enable his spirit, his consciousness to be transferred intact.

The idea to kill Michael had only come to him that morning when he had opened his mail and read the report about Judy and Michael that the private detective had sent him. The opportunity was too good to miss and it would be so easy to attribute the motive for his suicide to recent events. Alternatively he may decide to cast the blame on David who perhaps acted out of revenge after having discovered that Judy was having an affair with Michael. That way he would kill two birds with one stone, removing Michael from the equation and at the same time discrediting David. Then the rewards would be his entirely.

Even if the police were too stupid to draw those conclusions themselves, Jonas could always give them the little package he had hidden in his safe. He chuckled to himself as he dragged David's comatosed form into a satisfactory position and managed to heave it onto the waiting bed. Then he quickly made the connections necessary to monitor his spirit's transition from this world to the next. In a lumbering shuffle he moved his corpulent form rapidly across the room to deal with the girl. He had not killed her, only administered a knock out dose of a less powerful drug combined with an amnesiac that would erase her memory of these events. Although a big man he struggled with the limp form, bloated at this late stage of pregnancy, but eventually managed to lift her onto the bed. Now he went to the terminal and carefully, with the unhurried precision of one devoid of conscience, he activated the audio interface and began his interrogation of the computer.

"Status of donor?"

"Comatosed. Subject's cerebral cortex still active but overall brain function decreasing. Estimated full brain shut down in thirty seconds and counting, twenty nine..."

"Status of recipient?"

"Recipient's condition stable, foetal heartbeat within limits."

"Emit particles and adjust bias."

For a fraction of a second a faint crackle accompanied the luminescence that followed. Then as the bias was reduced the blue-ish haze melted.

"Fifteen, fourteen...."

Jonas waited, excitement mounting.

"Commence recording."

"Recorders already active. Professor Hawkin's instruction were to maintain twenty four hour recording within the chamber."

"What..." Jonas stammered. His jowls quivered as his head turned quickly to stare into the single eye of the camera pointed directly at him. "You mean everything that has occurred is on record?"

"Confirmed. Seven, six...."

Mentally Jonas made a note to do something about the recordings. For the moment that would have to wait, he told himself. He must see this through first. In an increased state of agitation he turned as if to reassure himself that the girl was still there. Satisfied he brought his attention back quickly to David's limp form.

"Brain shutdown has occurred, monitoring elapsed time...three, four.."

Jonas held his breath for what seemed an eternity then

145

a slight crackle and the blue-ish haze returned. At first there was just a pinpoint of light above David's head then almost imperceptibly it began to expand and fill.

He released his pent up breath and wiped nervously at his forehead. Staring intently at the growing spirit he was totally unaware that the same thing was happening behind him and with cold indifference had not even considered the matter of Michael's death or where his spirit might go.

The blue cloud was full and gently tore itself away from its position above David's head. The atmosphere was electric and Jonas stared in almost disbelief as the spirit floated across the room.

Behind him another was growing above the forehead of Michael. As it filled so the imbalance of the bias was created. The equipment had been set to handle the emergence of just one spirit and Jonas was unaware of the fast approaching critical stage of the bias.

There was a crash. Jonas staggered back as the entire room flashed blue for a second when all the particles in the room were simultaneously illuminated. Automatically he lifted his hand to shield his eyes but almost instantly the blue-ish haze subsided.

Then there was nothing to be seen.

Jonas fidgeted nervously.

He spun around to locate the missing spirit but with no success. It was then he saw Michael's body and a sense of discomfort struck him as he noticed the eyes of the dead man staring straight at him.

He waited for David's spirit to reappear, to see it enter Judy. The minutes ticked by, minutes that seemed like hours.

Nothing.

Finally and with uncertainty as to what had actually happened, he made his way to a couch and lowered his body. He needed time to think.

Had the transfer taken place? He asked himself.

It must have done, he decided. He saw it hovering above the girl. He didn't actually see it enter her body as he had expected but that must have taken place when the big flash of light blinded him. Yes, he assured himself, it must have gone to plan.

He looked around the room and made out the forms of the two dead men. David's screwed up features bore witness to his sudden death. The pain filled expression and the mouth still bearing that last anguished grimace were made more horrible by the disease ravaged body.

Michael's eyes were still open and seemed to be staring at him with accusation. They were dead eyes, empty somehow. He turned away, his stomach heaving with disgust.

They were the first corpses he had ever seen and he was unnerved. Death was a stranger, uglier than he had expected. The whole aura of the room was somehow macabre and he suddenly wanted to get out of there very quickly. Still breathing rapidly he shuffled to his feet and made his way over to David's body. He pulled the document that David had signed that morning from his pocket and carefully unfolded it then deposited it on the table beside the bed on which David's corpse lay.

He avoided looking into the open staring eyes as he uncurled the fingers and slowly wrapped them round the empty syringe that he had used to inject the drugs assisting the complete spirit transfer.

STILLBORN

Then after a brief check on Judy's condition he left quickly, moving his huge body with surprising speed back to his own office to make the necessary calls that would constitute the next phase of his plan.

He was sweating profusely from the physical exertion and from the nervousness that he felt. He collapsed into his chair gratefully and allowed himself a few moments in which to recover his poise before collecting his thoughts and continuing to administer his plans.

As his breathing slowed his anxiety was replaced with a feeling of self satisfaction. All in all, he decided, it had gone very well. He was particularly pleased with his own performance. He reached down into his desk draw and pulled out a bottle of whiskey. He needed a drink, he felt he had earned one.

The exact moment of death was easy to pinpoint.

There was a flash of brilliant white light and at that moment time seemed to stand still.

The memories of many lifetimes cascaded through his consciousness, startling him with their clarity and profusion.

In awe he realised that there was no room for fear, only love. He was safe and warm and above all else he was free.

Free in a way he would never have believed possible. Time seemed to lose all meaning, becoming three dimensional and surrounding him. He suddenly realised that he had stepped through the door that was mortality.

The door closed with a solid clunk that inferred finality but then he realised that it didn't matter, he was still alive.

At least he had a feeling of being alive but in reality his consciousness was now existing at a level that was quite different to being alive. The only comparison to normal human sensation was with dreaming, feelings one associated with consciousness had been suddenly and distinctly cut off. He had no apparent physical senses such as sight, sound or touch, yet at the same time he was aware of those faculties but at a different level. It was like cinema, remote and somehow unreal, as if viewed through another's eyes in the way one experienced a vivid dream.

There was sight but it did not come from his eyes rather it just existed within his being, there was sound but without the source of ears and there was a sense of feeling in that he experienced the comfort of warmth although even this did not originate from nerve ends on the surface of his skin. But then the contents of a dream were not seen, heard or felt but merely experienced within the mind. So this state in which he now existed was similar and was certainly dreamlike. But dreams are not reality so how could he be sure that there was any substance in these present sensations; that these were not just the last few milliseconds of life in which a lifetime's experiences had been compressed haphazardly. For a brief second the comforting warmth gave way to a chilly wind and as if that was possible he felt a shiver pass through him. Then as these uncertainties faded he felt warm and safe once more as he continued his journey into the unknown.

First of all Jonas called for help and the immediate assistance he needed was that of his technicians in ensuring that Judy was looked after and that "his" experiment was safe. He regarded the whole program as his now. Why shouldn't he? He asked himself. After all it was the dedicated work of his department that had resulted in this discovery. It was he, Jonas, who employed these people and sanctioned their work and now it was he that was left to see it through, he was the only person left with a full knowledge of what was taking place within that chamber just yards away from where he sat.

As the recent memories of the dead people evaporated, Jonas began to feel pleased with himself. The whiskey helped too. He picked up his glass and after offering himself a salute of admiration, he swallowed the last mouthful and felt ready to proceed with his plan.

He called his two most able members of the technical staff and seconded an eminent gynaecologist from the medical department and arranged for them to report to him immediately.

His next step was the most loathsome but one that couldn't be avoided. With a shrug he called the local police station. He asked for Chief Superintendent Blake, a man he had met at some function or other. The superintendent told Jonas his officers would be on the scene as soon as possible and to avoid touching any of the evidence.

Quickly anticipating the arrival of his staff and the police, Jonas reached down into a draw and grabbed a tranquilliser which he swallowed quickly. Then he got up from his desk and lumbered into his bathroom and quickly splashed his face with cold water. Standing up straight he brushed what hair he had back neatly and looked at himself in the mirror. His reflection reassured him. He gazed into his own eyes

with satisfaction bordering on self adulation and felt
confident that he could carry this through without any
difficulty.

STILLBORN

CHAPTER ELEVEN

George Baxter was the DCI who headed up murder investigations. He had come along to the CDG laboratories to have a look around after reading the SOCO report and following a telephone call from Superintendent Blake.

'Go Easy', he'd been told. 'I know the department head.'

Well sod that, he thought, I'll do it my way or not at all. Which is probably why he hadn't been promoted to Superintendent. He'd put in the time and scored enough brownie points but diplomacy wasn't in his vocabulary..

"I don't like this Len!" He said emphatically. "Two of them dead, the pregnant woman was found unconscious. The only one still on his feet is this Nichols character."

"There are quite a few others here guv"

"Yes but not in this department. Anyway there's something about him I don't like...I've met him before you know."

"Yeah. Where was that then?"

"Some civic do, he knows the Super too."

"Oh."

"Nichols phoned him up, reported the deaths to him. The Super told me to take it easy on him."

Len looked over at his boss, a little sneer on his face. "That was a mistake."

"That's right son. First thing that gets me going is when someone starts telling me how to do my job. I've been doing it bloody long enough."

"Do you think he's involved?"

"I don't know, do I? We only just got here. Not even sure its a murder yet except that there's two of 'em," he paused, like a hunting dog his nose quivered as if he was trying to pick up clues just by sniffing the air. "You do though don't you guv? I've seen that look on your face before."

"You wait till you see him. Must weigh nearly twenty stone." Sergeant Len Brown stifled a yawn and tried to look interested.

"All that gear in there. SOCO tried to send the woman off in an ambulance but he stopped them, said their own medics would look after her. No, there's definitely something very odd been going on around here, he's hiding something....I'm sure of that." George stopped talking for a minute as if to give the problem some more thought. Then leaning towards the sergeant he added.

"What about that woman eh? They've got her under sedation, I bet she knows plenty about this. Hummm...two dead men and an unconscious pregnant woman. You just make sure the forensic people cover every square inch of that laboratory," he stood up abruptly, causing Len to jump.

"I'm going to get to the bottom of this Len."

George turned and strode out of the laboratory leaving Len looking at his back and wondering what to do next.

Of course he wasn't the only one that didn't know what to do next. George had been a DCI for over ten years and during all that time there was one thing he had learned and that was not to expect anything except the unexpected. Each case was like a story, you just had to keep turning pages to get the answers. George was pleased that this one had landed on his lap, he hadn't had a tasty investigation to get his teeth into for some time.

The younger DI's got most of the action these days, somehow George Baxter seemed to pick up all the Community Liaison rubbish or dealing with this committee or that reporter.

'All the bloody paper work too!' He muttered as he gently prodded a few items lying on the desk. He was bored with his role as DCI which seemed to have very little to do with police work these days.

Admittedly he wasn't as young as he used to be and in his current position of seniority one would expect a certain amount of politics and paper work. The thing that annoyed George was that he was better with 'hands on' work, better than a lot of the young DCI's who were trying to make a name for themselves.

All he did was parade around, attend functions and molly coddle some pompous dignitary or other.

He guessed that was why Blake had given him this one, didn't think it would become a full blown murder investigation, just a bit of PR and gently, gently stuff.

'Well fuck him' he muttered. 'Let's see what shit there is to stir.'

At last he felt he had something to get his teeth into, some real police work to do and he would do it properly, efficiently, even ruthlessly if necessary. He was determined about that. Retirement might be looming but he would make sure they didn't forget him in a hurry. 'Bastards!'

He marched into reception and asked to see Jonas. Sitting there thinking about it, he put together the little he knew. First there was the professor lying on an operating table, stone dead and with a surprised look in his eyes. Well, he thought, the guy was so skinny he looked like a corpse anyway. He would have believed that it was natural causes if it wasn't for the evidence and the other two.

Then there was the big one with the foreign name. That one looked a hard case and judging from his physique he definitely hadn't died of natural causes. You only had to look at the way he was lying there with his hand outstretched, as if he was trying to grab hold of something, to realise that there was something suspicious about his death.

Lastly the woman. He didn't know what she had been doing in there because those damned technicians and the doctor had admitted that they had moved her into the next room. Ought to be hauled in for tampering with evidence in his opinion.

"Mr Nichol s will see you now."

"Will he?, that's bloody good of him," muttered George stamping into Jonas' suite and helping himself to a chair.

Jonas looked at the man with distaste and found it hard to stop himself saying something that he would regret. The policeman's whole attitude was insolent, the way he had swaggered in and made himself at home. With an effort he adopted his diplomatic guise and kept his anger in check.

"How can I help you, er.."

"Detective Chief Inspector Baxter. First of all you can tell me how you came to have two dead men and an unconscious woman lying around in one of your laboratories?" The irony was heavy in his voice and the inspector sneered at Jonas as he spoke.

"Do you think this happens every day around here?" Jonas felt his anger rising. He wasn't used to people talking to him in this way, being a department head at CDG he commanded respect. "Two of my colleagues are found dead including a well respected professor who was a personal friend of mine and you charge in here as if you own the place and start asking ridiculous questions."

"Ok take it easy. We all have our own responsibilities and mine is to get to the bottom of this mess as soon as possible," he paused for emphasis and allowed the sneer to form on his lips again. "So I hope you will pardon me if I cut the crap and get straight to the point."

"David Hawkin and his assistant were involved in research of a very sensitive nature. I'm afraid I will need clearance from our board before I'm allowed to divulge any details of the work in which my department was involved. I will also need your own assurances that anything I do say to you will go no further. I mean no further too, it mustn't even leave this room!"

"Look Nichols I don't care who the bloody hell you are or how sensitive your work here is. I'm investigating a possible double murder! You get in my way and I'll have you behind bars for obstruction or withholding evidence. It's your choice!"

"I will answer any questions except those related to the research being carried out here. You will have to wait if you need information about the professor's work, do you understand!" Jonas's jowls shook as he spoke, his complexion darkened. Both anger and fear were working on him but anger still had the upper hand. Jonas had a big ego, it wasn't to be crushed that easily.

"Yes I understand very well, but let me make

something quite clear to you. I could take you back
to headquarters right now for questioning,"
He's bluffing, thought Jonas smugly, he wouldn't
dare.
"..but for now I will accept that your work may have
confidential aspects. I'll play it your way, just this
once. You have twenty four hours to get clearance
then I will want all the answers." George stood up
red faced and glared at Jonas. Jonas allowed a little
smirk to light up his face but said nothing.
"Make no mistake! I intend to get to the bottom of
this!" George turned abruptly and stormed out of the
office.
Jonas congratulated himself on how he had handled
the policeman.
George muttered to himself as he marched out and
his look conveyed the anger he was feeling. Perhaps
Jonas should not have alienated this man, George
Baxter was not a very nice man when crossed.
Twenty years earlier George Baxter had been on his
way up through the ranks. He was known to be hard
but fair, his team respected him and so did the
villains.
George knew that to the rest of them he was really a
symbol, a reminder of days gone by and perhaps he
did not really fit into today's sophisticated police
force. He hadn't joined up to learn how to operate a
computer or get onto committees. His interest had
been in catching the crooks and putting them away
and he had been good at it.
George had arrived back at the station. He got out of
the car and made his way to his office where he sat
thoughtfully considering the matter.
Really there was not much that he could do until Len

returned with the results from the forensic tests.

This was frustrating for George and so to occupy himself he made a few calls to try and find out what he could about CDG and what they could possibly have been up to in that laboratory.

David was in no man's land, out of his old body and waiting for a new one.

The passage of time was incalculable for he had no reference upon which to base any estimation. Disconnected as he was from physical being he had no biological timepiece to refer to, not even the finite pulsing of his heart.

His thoughts, if they could be called that, did not rely upon the mechanics of the brain, upon electrical signals conducted through nerve fibre or any other limitation of his former being. In his current state a hundred years could flash by in an instant or a second seem like eternity.

There was nothing David could do to alter his situation. Certainly his memory seemed unimpaired, he was aware of who he was and what he was doing there. His ability to observe and to remember seemed unchanged. There was however, something fundamental missing, something that he would have noticed if he had been able to consider this in a mortal way.

It was something that even with all their preparation and research they had not considered.

David could no longer think.

Thinking was a simple mechanical process which required the use of a brain. Thought or sentience seemed to have happened in humans by accident. It was arguably the single factor that had led to the dramatic evolution of their species yet at the same time was responsible for hiding from them real knowledge of their condition.

Thinking was carried out by the brain. The brain had been part of David Hawkin, the physical being that his spirit had inhabited. Now he was pure spirit, had no brain, could not think.

He did not even have the simple mechanical inter-faces of sight, hearing or touch either. Now he only had awareness which seemed strange to him even though it had always been the basis of his being.

Awareness seemed new to him, a sense he had all but forgotten how to use. It was the core program upon which all the other layers of intelligence had depended.

The closest we come to it is when we are asleep.

So David existed now in a state that could only be compared with dreaming, but just like all dreams its feeling of reality was total.

That was being aware.

Immediately after death it seemed as if he was slowly floating away from his body. After an indeterminate period of time he was aware that his journey was coming to an end. During that journey, while in a molecular form, he had felt as if was surrounded by a very white pure light that billowed like cumulus cloud on a sunny day. He was aware of a comforting warmth, he sensed a motion which was soft and undulating, like a sail-boat on a pond with only a gentle breeze to move it along. All the time he was conscious of the perfection of his environment and how during that brief journey between death and life, while being devoid of physical sensation, he had acquired a feeling of utter security and safety. Perhaps, he imagined, those who returned from the

very jaws of death had shared a little of this sensation, having at least looked into this tunnel of light
before returning to their earthly shell. The sensation
of freedom was so acute, the perspective of physical
being was so different that he began to wish that he
did not have to return to the confines of a human body
at all.
Just as abruptly as the journey had begun and his
connection with the mortal world had been severed,
so just as suddenly his passage seemed to be coming
to an end and struggle as he might to avoid leaving
the warmth of his spiritual cocoon, he began to
perceive the return of physical sensation.

The board had reconvened at Jonas's request and once
again the twelve pairs of eyes stared accusingly in
his direction.
"The whole matter of the deaths that occurred is
distressing to us all, to none more than myself. I have
lost not only two invaluable members of my staff but
two very good friends." Jonas emphasised the word
'friends'.
Standing at the end of the boardroom table and leaning forwards, his hands gripping the table's edge, he
adopted what he hoped was an expression of distress.
"Gentlemen. What I have come to tell you now is of
monumental importance to us all."
He stopped and cleared his throat for effect.
"I....I mean we, have been involved in proving a
theory that will astound you . I have here the proof,
the results of countless experiments," He tapped his
brief case emphatically, "This will change the
meaning of life as we know it."
"Even now the final experiment continues. The

results will confirm everything that I am about to tell you and will prove that we have uncovered something very important. For want of a better title, let me call it the secret of....." Once again he paused and scanned the eyes that regarded him with such suspicion. "Eternal life!"

There were gasps and shouts of disbelief and all at once questions and suggestions were being fired in all directions. "Gentlemen.....Gentlemen, please!"

All conversation ceased and for once they awaited his words, some in disbelief others hoping that they had heard correctly. After all, Jonas thought, they were all old men and his decision to tell them this was based on the fact that they, of all people, needed what he now controlled. Subconsciously he sneered. 'Look at them now', he derided. 'Drowning men clutching at straws. Helplessly feeding out of my hands.'

"Please gentlemen! Let me continue."

Continue he did and during the next hour hardly a word was spoken as he explained, clarified and delivered a memorable oration on the reincarnation program. Hungrily they listened, doubters rapidly became believers as he distributed articles and reports supporting what he was saying. Finally, when he had finished, he sat down and sipped his glass of water as he was assaulted by a barrage of questions. Eventually all the questions were answered and the twelve men were now satisfied that Jonas had indeed brought them amazing news and they were congratulating him and themselves.

Carried away as they were by the euphoria of the moment, they had completely lost sight of the issue of why Jonas was there in the first place. They didn't even question the fact that he had previously hidden this from them.

That is all except the chairman who was now calling them to order and with a suitably sombre expression began addressing Jonas.

"Thank you Jonas for having been so candid with us. We appreciate the importance of the work in which your department is involved but what of the deaths of these two men, your professor and his assistant? What can you tell us of this?"

"Not a lot at this stage John. From the note he left it seems that the professor was close to death anyway and in order to save the time that would be involved in seeking the approval of the BMA. he went ahead and become the donor in a human test. Obviously I do not approve of the rashness of his actions but it will save considerable time and I have now taken all steps to protect the integrity of the experiment. As for the other man, his assistant, I think there must be some connection but we don't have the complete picture at this stage.

The main problem that I can foresee is in protecting the project from outside interference. I have already been subjected to numerous questions by the police and felt unable to provide all the information they required without disclosing the delicate nature of the project itself. There will be more questions and I do feel that I need the full support of the board in maintaining confidentiality."

"I suppose we will have to wait for the outcome of the investigation by the police before we really understand what took place. I am also sure that you have the full support of the board if you feel that you need it Jonas. Is there anything in particular that we

162

can do at this stage?"

"Yes there is. I'm glad you have raised the matter. The police are going to push for answers and I told them I needed clearance from you because of the confidential nature of the research.

The inspector has suggested that I could be charged with obstructing justice. I would therefore ask you to give me the necessary backing in my refusal to answer any questions about the project to which we are committed.

Perhaps some of you may be in a position to apply some discreet pressure on Inspector Baxter to respect our wishes in this matter."

For a few minutes there was silence around the table and Jonas feared that he may have over stepped the mark. This was certainly a delicate matter but he felt sure that they could still see the carrot that he had dangled firmly in front of them and would use their power and influence to help him.

Sir Gerald Ogilvy turned and whispered to a colleague then leaned forward and consulted the chairman. As they spoke in whispers there were several glances in Jonas's direction.

"Gentlemen," the chairman looked around at the other members, "In view of the extremely valuable work of Jonas' department, which I feel we must protect at all costs, I propose we give him the kind of support he is seeking. Sir Gerald knows the Commissioner and says he will make contact and hopefully a bit of pressure will be applied, someone will have a quiet word with this troublesome inspector. If anyone else can contribute I suggest you discuss it in private with Sir Gerald."

Jonas smiled to himself. Not only had the board fallen

hook, line and sinker for the project, but with their contacts at the right levels, he felt confident that he could ensure that the insidious George Baxter didn't give him too much trouble.

"Thank you for your support gentlemen. If there are no other matters I would ask your leave so that I can get back to my laboratory?"

"Certainly Jonas and please do not hesitate to call me if I can be of any further help. Good luck and keep me posted on any developments."

"Thank you."

Jonas rose and made a rapid departure, the contrite expression on his face hiding his sense of achievement and growing self esteem.

Judy sipped the drink that was handed to her and once again demanded to know what was going on.

"Where are David and Michael? Look doctor, I've been lying here all day on my own. When will someone tell me what happened. Did I faint?"

"Relax Judy. Your questions will be answered soon enough, just rest and think of your baby. Have you felt it move?"

"Funnily enough it really did kick just as I started to come round. It felt as though somebody was chasing it around inside me. I suppose it was something to do with me fainting....... doctor, can't you please tell me what is going on?"

"No Judy. I don't know any more than you do except that you will be having your baby very soon."

"What do you mean? Has it started? I don't think I've felt any contractions yet."

"No, Judy," he patted her gently on the arm. "Don't worry. It won't be for a few days yet."

"But what about David. The experiment....

tomorrow......."

She pushed his arm off and sat up agitatedly.

"I can't tell you anything. Mr Nichols said....."

"What has it got to do with him. David said that Michael would be looking after me, after he... ," anxiously she grabbed at him. "What is going on? Where is Michael?"

The doctor didn't know what to say. He was just as ill at ease as everybody else over the matter of these deaths.

"Look Judy I am just not allowed to tell you any more even if I knew it. I'm on strict instructions, my job is to look after you. If you don't relax and stop working yourself up into a state I'm going to have to give you another sedative."

Judy lay back, defeated.

"Ok doctor, you win."

"Good I'll look in again soon after you have had your supper. Try to relax."

She had already made up her mind what she was going to do as soon as he had gone. She got out of bed and pulled a robe around her then carefully made her way to the door. Placing her fingers on the handle she turned and pulled it gently. Nothing happened, the door was locked.

"Oh damn you!" She cried, shaking the door as she burst into tears.

The door opened and a stout nurse took hold of her arm.

"Come on my dear. Back to bed or I will have to call the doctor."

"Call the damn doctor," she yelled in frustration.

Then with little alternative she made her way back to bed and lay down. She buried her face in the pillow

STILLBORN

and started sobbing quietly.
"Oh Michael. Please come."

CHAPTER TWELVE

David knew that the transfer was complete as he slowly became aware of physical sensation returning. It didn't happen suddenly or dramatically, it wasn't as if he was travelling within that shaft of white light when with a flash of lightning and a crash of thunder he felt his being deposited within a living organism. It was more like waking up in a strange bed, although for David it was a strange body. His recent experiences had that unreal quality of a nightmare but as he tried to evaluate his current circumstances the dream faded into the recesses of his mind.

The very first sensation was of movement. He felt himself slipping and sliding within the amniotic fluid although complete awareness of his situation did not occur at once. He couldn't see. He was not even aware of his eyes and although muted sounds somehow reached his brain, he couldn't locate the source or even define how that sensation of sound reached him. He was vaguely aware of the form he occupied but the underdeveloped nervous system was sending its signals in a fairly haphazard way to a brain that was not yet fully programmed to interpret them. The feeling of warmth and security that had surrounded him as he travelled through the tunnel of light remained, but it had become a more physical sensation, not quite as abstract as it had been.

The most frightening thing that was happening to him was a feeling of being half in and half out of a dream. He couldn't quite focus his mind or distinguish between the mental pictures being created in his new brain and the spiritual images that he had so recently experienced. His earlier determination to mentally record everything that was occurring seemed to slip away and try as he would he could not seem to retain any memory of events as they passed him by. He tried very hard to recollect the journey through death into life again, but could only summon up hazy images.

Like a person suffering from a serious head injury, he felt himself slipping from consciousness into oblivion and back again without ever attaining any mental clarity or being able to focus his powers of reason. He supposed that he was sleeping most of the time like any other foetus. Even when he was awake he felt very tired and he had that warm and secure feeling that encouraged sleep. He didn't worry too much about this, indeed he couldn't have done anything about it even if he wanted to. But more than that, he had no inclination to fight that overpowering lethargy but was happy to submit almost benignly to this present, very comfortable state of semiconsciousness.

He soon realised that an awareness of time had come back to him and the pervading rhythm of his pulse frightened him at first. He could feel the small heart beating away and would lie for long periods just listening to its erratic pattern, worried by the constant changing of pace and knowing his new life depended on it. It seemed so weak and uncertain. Sometimes as he was concentrating on the fluttering within him it would stop for several seconds and he would know fear, a real human emotion that filled his little body with uncertainty. Then just as unpredictably it would begin again and he would feel his anxiety drain away.

Each time he woke he became aware of a little more, there would be some subtle increase in physical sensation. His nervous system was developing rapidly and he was becoming more and more acclimatized to his new body.

Time was still difficult to assess, he couldn't tell whether minutes or hours had passed since he had occupied his new body because he had nothing to tell him how long he slept, although he guessed it was most of the time. Neither was there any day or night in his little cocoon and no timepiece to guide him other than his own erratic heartbeat and the movements of his mother.

Mental processes were difficult, his thoughts were blurred and hard to discipline. It seemed as if the brain he occupied was not quite ready for the invasion of his intellect. He thought vaguely about where he was and created an image in his mind of his mother, a picture that was a combination of his own natural mother in his previous life and of Judy. The thought that he was inside Judy's body didn't cause him any uneasiness but rather the reverse. He felt a warm glow and tried to distinguish whether this was because of his feelings for Judy or a bonding process that was taking place between himself, as the baby, and Judy, the mother in whose body he now lived.

As feeling increased and his mind became clearer, he began experimenting with his new body. He forced his mind to evaluate his physical sensations and as he became vaguely aware of his limbs, he tried to move them with varying degrees of success. It seemed that they moved spasmodically, almost of their own accord and he decided that he would obviously have to learn how to control his new body from scratch.

STILLBORN

He wondered whether he would learn this more quickly than a normal baby or whether it would take him a year before he took his first faltering steps. How long would it be, he wondered, before he would conquer speech and before he could communicate with the outside world. He had considered this matter during the run up to the transfer and had concluded that it should be possible to achieve adequate results in a much shorter time than usual. Indeed, the experiments that he had carried out on the monkeys had suggested that when memory was retained, mental agility and learning were developed much more rapidly. His research had been based on animals and the results might not apply to him, humans could react very differently. Man had a much larger repertoire of skills and considering how much longer it took him to reach maturity, he may react very differently.

His current lack of physical control was a bit disquieting. What, he asked himself, if there is something wrong with my nervous system? What if I am to be born paralysed or can't communicate for some reason? The whole experiment will be a disaster. Then, as if on cue, he managed a vague response to a mental effort to move one of his little arms and he relaxed again.

So his first few hours were spent in accepting and learning to control the new body that he now occupied and because of the excitement of his transition and the fascination that he was now experiencing, he hadn't focused his attention on how, or why, his death had occurred so unexpectedly. As his development progressed and he spent more and more time in an ever increasing state of awareness, he would begin to remember with surprise that the experiment had begun ahead of schedule. He would start to wonder why this had happened and to consider the implications.

Very soon, he would become aware of other more frightening aspects of his new environment, of a vague feeling of intrusion into his world. He would sense too, the other problems that he had not expected to occur and as reality brought more physical awareness, so the problems that came with life would begin to erode his present feeling of security.

For the present at least, protected by the fluids within his mother's belly, he felt safe and happy.

"Ok Len, lets have a look at what we've got. On face value it looks as if David Hawkin poisoned Tamasoto and himself. His letter offers a sort of blanket acceptance of responsibility."

"Yep. May as well get it wrapped up then."

"No...no, not so quick. We know he had cancer, that's a good enough reason to top himself. Not for murder though, especially as they were supposed to be such good friends. What's the motive?"

"Its probably the woman, it's usually money or women. Anyway it doesn't really matter guv, he put his hands up to it."

"Len, sometimes I really wonder about you. Why did you want to be a policeman anyway?"

"Well..the pay, then there's job security."

"Shut up you bloody fool. Now listen to me, my instinct says its murder, we're not finished here yet. Let's start again. The note, what d'you make of it?"

"Well he admits it guv. Says it's all down to him."

"That's just it, he doesn't really. Clever bit of work that note, admits everything and nothing."

"Yeah, but."

"No Len. I've seen lots of these bloody things, people jumping off buildings, spreading themselves all over the pavement. Gassing themselves, even hanging themselves. They usually like to leave a note to tell the world what a bunch of bastards we are or how the missus was fucking a neighbour. People like to attribute blame. They don't want to die really, just want to make someone feel guilty and that's the only way left. They usually tried everything else and it didn't work."

"So..ok it seems a bit, y'know...thought out."

"You're catching on Len. This letter's a masterpiece. It's cold and clinical. The writer knew what he was doing and he wasn't about to kill himself."

"What?"

"Hawkin didn't write the note. He signed it alright, just didn't write the bloody thing."

"So if he didn't, who did guv?"

"Not sure yet. What do you think Len?"

"From what I've seen here so far guv, they're all a bit nuts. Spending all their time down here messing about with the occult and spirits and stuff. Perhaps it was some sort of suicide pact or a ritual of some kind that went wrong."

"No they don't tie in together. You know what I mean. Just look at them, a skinny little college professor and this yank, big chap too. No, I could go along with the professor killing himself but the Yank doesn't look the type. Much too physical."

George stared at the ceiling for a moment, his boots resting on David's desk.

"So what do you think?"

"That brings me to the next question Len. The

bubbly. What was that all about and tell me why four glasses had been used when there were only three of them there? It's my bet that Nichols was in on all this and I can't get anything out of him. He's got some powerful friends warning me off," he chuckled as if he was enjoying the fact that he was being pressurised from above. "They won't stop us eh Len? We'll get to the bottom of this little mess one way or the other. It's the big guy that's got the answers, that's my bet. He's the key."

"Well if you can't get him to answer your questions, what do we do next?"

"That's easy Len. We speak to the other one who was there at the time, the woman..... We must get to her without Nichols knowing, lean on her, get some answers and then we will have something to use on him."

George brought his feet down and leaned forward in his chair, his elbows resting on the desk. "What did we get from the autopsy report Len? Anything new there?"

"The times of death are the same within minutes. The professor was dying anyway, latter stages of cancer, probably only had a few weeks to live at most. I'm waiting for a full medical report, a Dr Bruce was looking after him, he's a cancer specialist.

The next thing was the position of the bodies. Forensic say the professor was moved, probably after taking the poison. The people here have already admitted that the pregnant woman was in the laboratory at the time of the deaths but they moved her out to look after her. I've checked her records and it seems that the professor had put her in the club, he was the father."

"Yes, that's a funny one isn't it. The woman is a beauty. Hard to imagine her and the professor screwing...... anything else?"

"Nothing that we haven't been over already guv."

"Right lets go and talk to the woman and see if we can get some answers."

George stood up abruptly and turned to leave the room. Len sighed. Being a lazy man he was in no hurry to accomplish anything. It really got to him when the boss was like this, all fired up and chasing around in every direction at once. He didn't care personally what George did, the problem was that he expected Len to do the same and Len knew that the next few days would be unbearable.

"Cocky shit!", he muttered to himself as he got up and followed George out.

"No. No I don't believe it," cried Judy. "Why Michael? Who would want to kill him?"

"Please don't upset yourself Judy. You knew David was going to end his life, does it really matter that much that he did it a day early?"

"Did.....they... do it?" She looked down at her swollen stomach and took her hands away frantically, "Is David in there?"

Jonas saw the look of horror spread across her face and realised it wasn't because David Hawkin had taken his life a day early. It was because of Michael Tamasoto, he obviously meant more to her than he had guessed. He leaned towards her with a smile on his face and grasped her hand but she immediately withdrew it and placed it once again on her stomach in a defensive way.

"You haven't answered!" She screamed at him. "Did

the transfer take place? Is he....David in there?"

"Yes, yes. Don't worry. Everything went according to plan. The transfer was complete, I was there, I saw to it."

"But what were you doing? I mean how did Michael ...die?"

"I'm just as much in the dark as you are as to what actually took place. Do you remember us toasting David and wishing him good luck?"

"No, not clearly, its all hazy."

"Well that's when it all started to go wrong. The three of you collapsed, either David or Tamasoto must have drugged the drinks. Which ever one it was nearly ruined everything and I can't think why they would have done it anyway. They were close friends weren't they?"

"Yes..we..all were."

He watched her closely to see what she would give away.

"Anyway I realised immediately what was happening and acted to make sure the transfer went ahead according to plan."

"You were here all the time, you saw...?"

"Yes fortunately I was or the whole thing would have gone wrong. I make it my business to keep myself up to date with the department's work and knew what the procedure was. I performed the transfer."

"And you are sure that David's spirit was definitely transferred into...my baby?"

"Yes, I saw it happen, you can relax?"

"Relax!" She yelled. "How can I relax knowing he is inside my baby's head and Michael is dead!"

She stopped abruptly, realising what she had said but she knew immediately that it was too late. She saw the sneer, the derision in his expression. She knew what he thought about foreigners. For a moment Judy chewed her finger as if in deep thought then suddenly she seemed to crumble in front of him. Tears trickled down her cheek and she began to shake.

"I don't want him in there!" She screamed. "I hate him! Michael said he wouldn't let it happen!"

Her entire body erupted in a fit of convulsions as she sobbed uncontrollably and with her clenched fists started striking at the mound in her belly. Jonas moved forward with surprising agility and grasped both of her wrists in his large hands and stopped her hurting herself and more importantly to him, the baby.

"Doctor!", he yelled. "Doctor come quickly. Hurry, this woman needs sedation!"

The doctor emerged at a half run and instructed a nurse who quickly prepared a syringe which she passed to thim. As she held the woman's arm, he inserted the needle into a vein. Almost immediately she stopped shaking and slumped back onto her pillow.

"Is she conscious?"

"Yes. Its just a strong tranquilliser which will inhibit any further anxiety. She'll probably sleep in a while but in the meantime you can talk to her. Everything else is in order. There is no need to worry."

"Thank you doctor, you can leave us now. I'll call if I need you."

"Certainly."

Judy opened her eyes and stared at him. The doctor withdrew and the nurse went about her business. Jonas waited a few moments, aware of Judy's eyes watching him. He considered her reaction to the news of the deaths and decided that his suspicions were correct, her involvement with Michael had obviously been a lot deeper than he had realised. She wasn't grieving for David, she was upset because Michael had died. Jonas made a decision, decided how he could use this knowledge to his own advantage. He leant forward and spoke in a conspiratorial whisper.

"Listen Judy. I know about you and Michael."

Her eyes widened a fraction but she made no comment, did nothing to interrupt his words.

"My main concern now is the transfer experiment and you of course. There will be a lot of questions from the police and I want you to think about your answers carefully. Do you understand?"

She nodded imperceptibly, her gaze still fixed on his eyes.

"It seems to me that David found out about you and Michael. Now I don't know what actually took place, maybe David took matters into his own hands or perhaps Michael himself accidentally or intentionally took the drug. What I'm saying is that it's in your own interest, and to safeguard the experiment, that none of this comes out. The last thing we want at this stage is for the police to take you away."

He paused and let his words sink in before continuing.

"As far as I'm concerned I don't know anything about you and Michael and I think it would be sensible for you to keep the matter to yourself as well. Do you agree?"

He stopped speaking and waited for her answer. When she did reply her voice was quiet, dispirited.

"Yes Mr Nichols, I understand." She closed her eyes and for a minute he thought that perhaps the sedative was making her sleepy but when he touched her arm they opened immediately and she stared back with that almost disinterested expression on her face.

"Jonas dear. You can call me Jonas."

She looked into his eyes and felt a twinge of fear or perhaps just uncertainty. She hadn't really paid him much attention in the past, he was just David's boss. Now as she looked into his cold eyes she felt hostility rise within her. She didn't know why but she wanted him to take his hands away and leave her alone.

"I'm tired now. Can you leave please?" She asked in a trembling voice.

"Good," he patted her hand and this time she did not resist. "You get some rest, I'll keep the police away from you for as long as possible, but prepare yourself for their questions, they can be quite direct. I think we understand each other, don't we?"

She didn't answer but Jonas knew he had her exactly where he wanted her. He turned to leave and his smile broadened. He was very pleased with himself.

As he walked down the corridor from the laboratory he passed David's office which had been seconded by the police. He wasn't surprised when he saw the inspector coming through the door and heading towards him.

"Ah Nichols, I'm glad I've run into you. I'm going to see the girl and then I want to go over a few things with you. Don't go anywhere for a while, clear?"

"I'm afraid you won't be able to question Judy for a while, the doctor has just sedated her. Its all been a bit too much for the poor girl, she has only just learned of the deaths."

"I suppose you told her?"

"Somebody had to and I thought it would be better

coming from me rather than from a stranger," he paused for a moment wondering how to deal with this arrogant man. However, at this precise moment Jonas was feeling buoyed up by how he had gained control over Judy and in his present state of mind, with his ego on a high, he felt magnanimous. Even towards the policeman.

He decided to be generous, to give the man some answers. He felt confident that he could control the outcome of these investigations.

"I think we got off on the wrong foot earlier inspector. Come back to my office now and I'll give you what ever help I can." Jonas smiled broadly, feeling very satisfied at how he was controlling events.

"Ok but I will need to see the woman sometime today."

"I'll have a word with the doctor and see what he says." Jonas turned and lumbered down the corridor towards his office with the two policemen in tow. Fortunately, following him as they were, they couldn't see the smile twist into a smirk or perhaps they would have been more sceptical about the sudden change in Jonas's attitude. Len had the mentality of a sheep and always looked with unerring faith to George for his lead, so it didn't strike him as strange that the big man seemed to have had a sudden change of heart. George on the other hand was less inclined to see the best in anyone and was already wondering what had made Jonas decide to help them. Cynically, he decided that the board had not been prepared to back him all the way. He knew from experience how loyalties tended to evaporate when people were dragged into something in order to protect a friend or colleague. Most people put their own welfare first and thought 'screw you'.

George knew the game as well as anyone and he decided to adopt a temporary change in attitude. Perhaps, he thought, the fat guy will give us more that way. If I creep a bit it may boost an already inflated ego and the fool will probably drop himself in it.

"Sit down gentlemen. Let me get you a drink. Coffee?"

"Coffee will be fine for us."

"Right. Now how can I help?"

The drinks were brought in and politely deposited within easy reach of the three men. George waited until Jonas's secretary had retreated and the door was closed firmly behind her. Then without giving an immediate response to Jonas's offer of help, he took a sip of his coffee. Replacing the cup he looked straight into Jonas's eyes and after silently holding his attention for a moment began speaking in an unusually mild and congenial tone of voice.

"Why don't you just tell us what you know and we'll go from there."

Jonas went over what had happened, avoiding any reference to specific details of David's work but at the same time admitting that the professor was involved in a major project which had been nearing its completion. He fed him other information that he was sure he would already possess, such as details of David's illness. He openly admitted his own presence in the laboratory at the time of the deaths of the two men. He apologised for not giving this information earlier but said that he felt duty bound to obtain clearance from the board before answering any questions that could have led to a breach of confidentiality. He laboured over the necessity to maintain secrecy over the exact nature of the work that was being carried out in the laboratory. Eventually, he felt as if he had provided a reasonable account of what he hoped they would believe had happened.

After pausing to sip his coffee once more, George began to ask his own questions and Jonas waited patiently for the other man to extract just the piece of information that he wished to part with and would appear to do so with great reluctance.

"So where does the woman fit in?"

"She was close to David Hawkin, they intended getting married, that is before he discovered that he was dying."

"She's just about to have a baby," George remarked with feigned surprise.

"Yes they seemed to have jumped the gun a bit but these things do happen, I suppose."

"Who is the father?"

"Well!....David Hawkin...I think,"

"Why 'think', could it be anybody else?"

"No...er no!", Jonas left just enough uncertainty in his voice to prise the next question from the policeman. His eyelids drooped halfway over his eyes but he was watching his adversary with an interest that his sleepy expression hid well.

"Come on...you know something else, don't you?"

"Well there had been rumours, you know, just office gossip....about Tamasoto and her."

"Oh! Just rumours are they?"

"Yes...yes. Well you know how it is, no smoke without fire, eh?"

"So you think something had been going on. Come

on, this could put a whole new light on these deaths."
"Yes....yes I see that now, but....I didn't want you to
get the wrong idea. I'm sure David Hawkin
wouldn't... he's not that sort of person, not a
vengeful man."
"So what you're saying is that Tamasoto and the girl
were putting it together behind the professor's back?"
Jonas kept his eyes lowered and shrugged, then as if
coming to a decision reluctantly, he reached down into
his desk drawer and pulled out the private detective's
file.
"I suppose you should have this. I had hoped..." he
handed the file over to the policeman who scanned
its contents briefly before staring back at Jonas.
"I could take you in for withholding evidence you
know?"
"Yes...I realise now....but I was only trying to
protect professor Hawkin's good name, I hadn't
really thought that he could have murdered...."
"Who said anything about him being a murderer?"
"No. Quite right. I just thought, well its pretty
obvious really."
"Is it?"
After a few moments silence in which George stared
at Jonas who in turn looked down at his hands in mock
humility, the inspector spoke again in his quiet voice.
"Is there anything else you'd like to tell me while
we're at it. Any other secrets you'd like to get off
your chest?"
"No. I don't think so."
"Ok. Well I have a few questions of my own, there
are a few loose ends, things that don't seem quite right
to me," George pursed his lips as if in thought.
"Why the celebration?"

"Excuse me?"

"The wine, why the wine?"

"Oh...that. It was just an impromptu thing. It was David's idea, he had something to tell us....about his work, some breakthrough."

"Which was what?"

"We didn't get that far. Maybe we will never know now. But he was close to something...... I tell you what I'll do. Leave that one with me, I'll study his work reports and see if I can give you some sort of answer. So long as it doesn't breach security."

"And you were there?"

"Yes I've already said so. David asked me to attend."

"Michael Tamasoto?"

"He was David's assistant and very closely involved in the project. And of course they were friends. It was natural that he was there."

"Yeah really good friends, Tamasoto was screwing the professor's fiancee."

"Yes...it seems so."

"The professor and Tamasoto socialised regularly?"

"Yes all of them. Michael Tamasoto and his wife, David and Judy. They were all pretty close."

George thought about that for a moment. Part of his mind was still suspicious of this man, wondering why he was being so helpful all of a sudden. He didn't realise the extent to which he was being fed information but it would probably occur to him later.

"What about the girl? Why was she there? I would have thought that with only a few days to go she'd be at home with her feet up."

"Yes."

"Well? Why have you kept her here? If she's going into labour, shouldn't she be in a hospital?"

183

"We have all the facilities here."

"Come on man. This isn't a frigging hospital..... or is this an employee benefit, babies delivered while you work?"

"No. No, of course not. It's all to do with the professor's work. She will be here for some time."

"But of course you can't tell me any more about that... Its confidential!"

"Yes, it is. Haven't I given you enough to be getting on with? I've said I will try to get clearance to tell you more."

"Yes you're probably right. Anyway I think you've told me all I need to know for now. I'm sure you have a lot of work to do. This business must have caused you a lot of problems and I must get back to my office, there is other work. Perhaps you could call the doctor for me, to see when I can interview the girl?"

"Straight away." Jonas called through to the laboratory.

"Doctor, how is the patient?"

"Fine Mr Nichols, she's sleeping at the moment. I am concerned though, its not good for her at this stage of her pregnancy to be undergoing so much stress. She only has a few days to go you know. I may have to slow things down."

"Good, I'm sure she's safe in your capable hands. Look I've got the police here, the inspector wants to ask her a few questions. When will she be able to be interviewed?"

"Is it really necessary? I would prefer you to leave it until after the birth."

Jonas looked across at George Baxter and shrugged. "It is important. I'm sure they will try not to cause her too much distress," He looked at George again, who nodded. "Can't you give her another sedative. Don't knock her out this time though?"

"I suppose I can if it's really necessary....At least wait until she wakes up. If they come to the laboratory some time this afternoon, she should be able to answer their questions then. But tell them to come and see me first. I want to make sure she is comfortable and relaxed." "Ok," George chipped in. "I'll be there about three."

"Thank you doctor," said Jonas. He switched off the telephone and looked across at the two policemen.

"Well, if that's all gentlemen?"

"Yes that's enough for now and thank you for your cooperation Mr Nichols."

After they had left Jonas congratulated himself on his performance. He pulled open his drawer and poured himself a large drink.

Outside George said quietly to Len, "What do you think of that?"

"He's changed his tune. I think we're getting somewhere now."

"Yes, so do I. But I wonder where exactly?"

STILLBORN

CHAPTER THIRTEEN

During the latter half of the current millennium, when people became so materialistic, many of the old spiritual beliefs were abandoned, cast off as primitive. Modern technology had replaced the old sciences and much that was valuable was lost forever. Even so some endured. Through the cataclysmic changes brought about by age of the automobile, the aeroplane, and now the computer, there still remained pockets of resistance where old beliefs were practised and passed down to future generations.

For some reason the East was more successful than the West in preserving such antiquities and at least modern communication allowed some visionaries travelling into the West to bring their ideas with them. Michael Tamasoto smuggled some of his grandfather's ideology into Great Britain. All his life he had followed the teachings of the Taoists, practised their skills as presented by his grandfather and later at the Dojo where he trained. The young Michael Tamasoto had learned from his grandfather much as he had done from his father before him. The skills had stood him in good stead at times of crisis when he summoned those unknown forces to his side and overcome adversity.

As Michael struggled to hold on to consciousness, he was aware of the paralysis that was engulfing his body. He understood what had happened but was still shocked to realise that his death was inevitable. The very best he could do was to delay it, to buy himself time to think and act. His brain screamed at him that he would die if he let his grip on reality fade and the only thing that helped him during those first moments were his love for Judy and his skills. His immediate target was Judy. Somehow he must overcome the forces of nature, he must pervert his destiny. In some way he must combine his skills and his knowledge to ensure that they existed together in the future.

He was perhaps the first man to die who knew for certain that his spirit would live on. It wasn't just belief but knowledge that guided him. But he also knew that his love for Judy would be lost together with his human memory. Unless.... Hope is a powerful catalyst. He must die, he accepted that...but if he could preserve his love....instil it somehow in his spiritual being. If necessary he would sacrifice some other part of his self, anything. He must either increase the capacity of that magnetic cloud that transported his soul or give up some part of himself to make room for his love. He must!

The average man would have succumbed within seconds to the effects of the drug that he had inadvertently taken.

As the drug suffused his body, Michael focused on Judy. He saw her slump onto the floor near the couch and quickly lose consciousness. He didn't bother to consider the implications, to wonder whether or not the same fate had taken Jonas and David. Immediately the distress signals reached his brain he concentrated all his efforts in maintaining that awareness.

In desperation his immune system ordered its armies into action. His over developed pituitary sent urgent messages through his endocrine system and enzymes and hormones were secreted in abnormal quantities in a vain attempt to protect his organs from the poison that had invaded his body. He fell to his knees, swayed for a few seconds then tipped forward until he was on all fours.

Natural antidotes desperately fought the poison itself and the ultimate weapon, his will, was intent on denying the drug its inevitable victim. One deep breath and he concentrated on the pit of his stomach. As he felt the power rushing through his body, he directed that power, sent it to already damaged nerve ends, forcing his limbs to move.

He looked up, saw Jonas struggling with David's body, saw the needle glint as Jonas slid it into a vein in David's arm and inject the drug that would maintain David's awareness through death. He would have given anything to have that needle in his own vein but he had only his will and a dying body, he had nothing to bargain with.

Jonas turned to the instruments and adjusted the bias to the light emitting particles that filled the room. Michael watched, unable to do anything to stop what was now about to happen.

His over loaded immune system surrendered the use of his arms and legs in an effort to preserve the integrity of his vital organs. Paralysed, he collapsed to the floor, eyes still riveted on what was happening to David's spirit. He took deep breaths, forcing the air into his lungs by practised control over the muscles in the pit of his stomach, in...out, in....out, he forced the life giving oxygen in, he exhaled the dead air; he summoned unknown reserves from within and from outside his body.

He realised that Judy was only sleeping, had been given a knock out drug only. Also realised that David was dead, the cloud of light that marked the departing soul now evident above his head.

He saw the spirit leave, start to travel slowly to where Judy lay. He then turned his will to other matters. Still unquestioning he accepted his own death but as the most recent memories flowed in cinema like form before his eyes he saw the result of his last five years work condense to form a single word.

Reincarnation.

He realised he only had seconds left when after a few more fluttering breaths the muscles controlling his breathing ceased operation. His chest lay still like that of a drowning man whose lungs have finally filled with water.

He buried the panic that stole into his mind, he made his heart keep beating, vainly pumping the remaining oxygen to his brain. He seemed to lose touch with his body. He knew the importance of this moment and knew also that his spiritual existence was assured but was unwilling to surrender his mortal feelings. He made a pact, a subconscious entry into a bizarre contract. He would surrender anything to maintain his knowledge of Judy. Vision faded as he slipped within himself. Outside stimulus disintegrated. At first the scene before him became hazy then disappeared completely as the failure of his sight accelerated until he saw only red cells swimming within the blood vessels of his retina. Then they too faded from red to crimson then darker still until black. A chink of light returned but it was not seen by his eyes, it landed directly in his mind, ethereal images swirled, shadows becoming brighter. The light grew, at first dull white and opaque, then becoming brighter and translucent. Fluffy white clouds moved languidly but as time passed they swirled, ever brighter. He felt himself moving into the vortex, entering that spiritual tunnel.

He was suddenly aware that his body had died and that now he existed only in spirit form, but he had achieved part of what he had set out to, he had preserved his feelings, his mortal memory of Judy.

He reached back with all his will, searching for her. Looking down he saw his old body beneath him and in that moment of time summoned all of his newly acquired spiritual strength.

As the last logical thoughts of his brain disappeared, in the instant when his spirit was being filled from his apparently dead body, he combined both his physical and spiritual selves. An observer would have seen a final movement, the dead man's lips peeled back in a silent scream as he ordered his love to live within his spirit through death and into life again.

Judy was lying quietly in her bed as a result of the sedative the doctor had given her. Her red rimmed eyes still bore a reminder of the tears that had descended uncontrollably down her cheeks.

Her sobbing was subdued now and because of the drugs she felt disassociated from her own sorrow, as if the tears and sobs were merely a reflex action.

She couldn't believe that Michael had gone, had left her alone with this monstrosity inside of her. The idea that David was existing within her womb, perhaps thinking of her and looking forward to his birth, appalled her. The compassion she had felt for him only a few days ago had turned into revulsion and she couldn't begin to reflect on what he had been to her just a few months ago.

It was his, David's fault. He still existed while

Michael had gone for ever; and it was directly because of David's work that she was now in this predicament. Within the turmoil of her mind she cursed him, imagining him already deep inside her belly, planning to possess her again.

Then there was that filthy creature Jonas Nichols. She had always held him at a distance, feeling his eyes on her and experiencing an uncertainty about the man for no apparent reason but which made goose pimples appear on her arms and the hair on her neck to stand on end.

Now she knew what he was. He had come to her and told her of the deaths and she had seen no remorse or sadness behind the mask, just concern for his own interests. He had touched her with his stubby pink fingers and warned her of what to say to the police. Well, she thought, I know exactly what I'll say. Exactly who I'll point the finger at. It was him, he was there and the only one not to be drugged. It was not only David, but also Jonas who had taken Michael from her.

Her anger rose and with it her determination increased. She swore that those responsible for her loss would be punished. She controlled her breathing with a strengthening of resolve to see that justice was done. She plucked a tissue from the box on the table and wiped her eyes, dabbing at the tears. She heard somebody coming through the door and pulled herself up by her elbows and made an effort to compose herself.

The man who walked towards her was tall, not young, but with an air of authority and strength about him and with a firm face and short cropped greying hair. His eyes locked with hers immediately he entered the room and she felt an involuntary shiver, sensing as only a woman could the coldness behind the smile and the cruelty that showed in the lines around his mouth.

"Hello Judy. I'm detective Chief Inspector George Baxter," he said flatly.

"This is Sgt Freeman," he gave a dismissive wave of his hand in the younger man's direction. George Baxter pulled up a chair and seated himself beside the bed while the subservient Len took up a sentry position behind him. Judy paid the younger man little attention as she waited for George to begin his questioning.

"You know why we are here. Quite a little mess isn't it?"

"The doctor told me you wanted to ask some questions," her eyes flickered to where the doctor was standing by a bench as if busying himself with something.

"Yes, well...the doctor said we could have a few minutes with you and its important that we get to the bottom of this," George paused while evaluating the woman and trying to decide on how best to proceed. It was obvious that the girl was near the edge. Should he push her or take the soft approach, he mused. Push her he decided.

"Tell me about Michael Tamasoto?" He snarled.

"Michael?" She felt control going as soon as his name passed her lips.

"What can I tell you, I...I don't know him that well."

"Oh come on. You can do better than that! We know all about your affair with him. Please don't treat me like a fool!" He almost shouted.

The doctor lifted his head from whatever he had been

studying and was about to intervene.

"We know all about your messy little affairs!"

"But I...we," she sobbed. "Oh God can't you leave him alone. Michael's dead...."

"I need to know who killed him. Quite frankly I couldn't give a shit who you screw around with, just don't even think about holding out on me."

"Mr Baxter, inspector. I don't think you should be doing this," interrupted the doctor.

"Listen!" Barked George rising from his seat and turning threateningly towards the doctor. "I'll do what ever I think is necessary to get the information I want. Now either shut up or I'll have Len here remove you from the room."

The doctor hesitated as if about to argue but facing this man he weakened and turned away. George spun back and stared at the girl.

"Talk!"

"Michael....I..I loved him. We..", she burst into tears, the sedative failing to control the state of her emotions.

George smiled and arrogantly tossed his head. The doctor rushed to his patient and even Len was shaken, uncertain of his role and unwilling to argue with George Baxter when he was like this.

"Did professor Hawkin know about you two?"

"No....No, I don't think so. He couldn't have."

"But if he did, perhaps he murdered your friend Tamasoto?"

"No!"

"How can you be sure?"

Her eyes flickered with uncertainty.

"Come on. Who else would benefit from these deaths?" "I.....Why not ask Jonas?"

STILLBORN

"Why him?"

"The...project. He's the only one left. That's all he cares about!"

The doctor was next to her now, about to protest again. Judy was sobbing and clung to his hands, he turned and his mouth opened but then he saw that cold glint in the police inspector's eyes and said nothing.

George sneered then turned away.

"Come on! That's all we need."

David knew something was wrong as sensation improved. He began to experience the first feelings in his stubby little fingers a couple of days after having taken up occupancy of his new body. As he drifted between sleep and awareness he definitely noticed the improvements that were taking place in his ability to decode the outside stimulus he was receiving. It was almost like wearing in a new pair of shoes and as the body seemed to fit him better he was beginning to feel more, hear more, even detected varying shades of darkness through his tightly lidded eyes.

It was his sense of touch that improved most noticeably even though he seemed to have little control over the actual movements that he made. It was really strange when he first became aware of the squishy walls of the womb as he moved within the amniotic fluid, it made him feel something like a surgeon must when he delves into a patient's body. It was a strange environment and took a while to get used to.

Like any creature that suddenly found itself in a different environment, he unconsciously took stock of his surroundings using all the senses that were available to him. He soon became used to the movements of Judy which were especially noticeable when she got out of bed. Then he would be subjected to a swaying, see-saw motion and sometimes when she sat or lay down again he would become trapped in an uncomfortable position, perhaps with his face wedged in a corner of her womb. When that happened he would kick out involuntarily until she changed position and he was more comfortable once again. Sometimes his hearing would detect gurgling sounds as food or liquid passed by while he was in a position where his ears were particularly close to her digestive tract. Lately he had realised that he could hear the muffled sound of Judy's voice as it permeated through her tissues but it was more like a dull roar than an audible conversation and he was unable to make out what was being said. Whether this was only because of the poor quality of the sound as it was carried through her tissues, or possibly because he had lost some of his linguistic abilities, he wasn't too certain.

He also become aware of the more positive rhythm of her heartbeat that contrasted with the tiny flutterings of his own and finding this particularly comforting, he would usually drift off into a peaceful sleep after only a very short period of time.

It wasn't all good though. Some things really frightened him like when he discovered that he was not alone. His stubby fingers reacted to the unexpected movement of something else that brushed against them. At first he assumed that some part of Judy's anatomy was touching him but it became increasingly obvious that he felt these things even when Judy was not moving herself and was probably sleeping. Also, the movements were too distinct, too positive to be only some passive tissue coming inadvertently into contact with his hand. It was when the sensitivity in his fingers had increased sufficiently that he became fully aware of another hand, of similar size to his own, its fingers interlacing his. He tried to rationalise at first and wasn't certain to start with as to whether or not it wasn't just his other hand; or was it really the hand of a twin? As he forced himself to evaluate more specifically the contact that he felt, he realised for certain he was not alone in Judy's womb. Like any being experiencing something new and unexpected, familiarity soon took away the edge of surprise and it wasn't too long before the puzzle became more academic than threatening.

Memory was still difficult to rely on. He knew who he was and vaguely how he had come to be here. He worked hard during his short periods of wakefulness to remember more details of his work. Like an amnesiac, memory seemed to return in unexpected blocks of visualisation and as each segment of his previous life came into focus, he found he was able to join elements of the puzzle together. Try as he might, he could not recall details of Judy's pregnancy. Had he seen her medical files? Surely he must have done. Was there no mention of a twin?

Then in natural progression a new question arose within his mind and one that he was slightly afraid to seek the answer to.

The thought stunned him.

Who was his twin?

If the professor had found out about Tamasoto having an affair with his girl, he probably did it."

"Yes, that's what we are supposed to think, a simple matter of the jealous 'husband' killing the wife's lover then committing suicide. Well, he was dying anyway, so why not? He had nothing to lose. It just seems to me that we've been led to that conclusion by Nichols." George scratched his head as he struggled to answer his own questions and then added quietly.

"Why all the wires and pipes? What did the girl mean about Nichols and the project?"

"I don't know guv."

"Read me the autopsy report on the professor again, the bit about the other drug."

Len's brow furrowed as he struggled with some of the more difficult words in the autopsy report. "As well as the drugs that resulted in the deaths of both victims, David Hawkin had been injected with a mixture of other substances including LSD," Len paused and looked towards the DCI, his expression one big question mark.

"LSD. Don't see much of that these days, people used to jump off the tops of buildings when they had been on Acid, thought they could fly. What does it say about the quantity?"

"Less than a normal dose. Apparently it was part of a cocktail. The lab boys couldn't identify the other drug that it was mixed with."

"Why inject him with drugs? Doesn't make sense."

"Shall I go on chief?"

Yes. Skip the rest of the details on the drugs used, don't understand that anyway."

"Injected by syringe into a vein in the left arm, probably at about the same time that the oral toxin was taken that resulted in death."

"That's it, that's the bit I wanted. If the professor

injected himself, he must have done it before drinking the wine. If it was taken after he drank the poison, he couldn't have administered it himself, someone else did!"

"Yeah but...."

"How long does the other stuff take to work, the poison?"

"Er..." Len looked through the pages he was holding. "Here it is...immediate paralysis, fraction of a second."

"The syringe he used was still in his hand when he was found. Someone wanted us to think he injected the other stuff into his arm but he couldn't have done unless he did it before he drank the poison. Would he walk around with a syringe in his hand while they were having a cosy drink?"

"No...I suppose not."

"He didn't inject it. Someone else did after he passed out and then put the syringe in his hand. Who else was there and not either dead or unconscious?"

"Nichols."

"Got it in one. What do we do now Len?"

"Go back and work on him some more."

"Yeah. It won't be easy though. It's all circumstantial so far and there's a lot that still supports the theory that Hawkin did it all. We need an edge."

"Where? What else is there guv?"

"Don't know yet but there is something, I can feel it. You and I are going back to that laboratory tonight when everybody is out of the way. We are going to have a good look round!"

CHAPTER FOURTEEN

During the last few days he had turned around completely. It wasn't any of his doing, just the result of small contractions of Judy's abdominal muscles. Being upside down didn't matter when she was lying down because he would at least be horizontal. It was when she stood up that he became aware of the blood rushing to his head and felt more like a bat than a human being. He didn't like it much in this position and hoped it wouldn't go on for too long but he was well aware that his having turned around was a sign of his forthcoming birth. This in itself was a mixed blessing. On one hand he was glad that he would soon escape from the confines of Judy's womb but on the other he had misgivings about the actual birth experience that he would have to go through.

It would also be a relief to escape being trapped in there with his brother though, he knew his twin was another male, it was instinctive knowledge without any supporting evidence. The early feelings of warmth and safety had worn off soon after he realised that he wasn't alone. Not only was it very confusing but he felt threatened by his unknown sibling who seemed to take every opportunity to poke him and disturb his sleep.

Memory had come flooding back and he was pleased by that but then he started reliving the day of his death and was frustrated because he didn't know why it had happened so unexpectedly. Luckily he wasn't aware of what had happened to Michael or Judy or he would have been even more worried, but after giving it a lot of thought he contented himself with the probability that Jonas and Michael had pre-empted the transfer to save him from having to end his own life.

So who was his twin? He wondered.

Could he possibly be imagining the presence of another being? Did his brother exist only in his own imagination, in his own mind or even worse, had another soul somehow entered the same body as him? On the other hand, if he accepted that he had a twin, then who could be occupying his sibling's body? The transfer would have taken place within the sealed chamber in the laboratory, so no other spirit could get in or out. That being the case, his twin probably had no soul, his own elaborate precautions had prevented this from happening.

Of course the fact that David in his disease ridden condition had succumbed so quickly to death, had prevented him from realising that he had not been alone, that indeed there was another whose spirit was not only available but was intent on joining Judy in death. There was one final possibility, his own spirit was divided between them both. This discomforting idea would in itself explain the difficulty he had in remembering certain things. Perhaps, he thought, that would explain the identical twin syndrome and how they seemed to have a higher level of communication and reliance upon each other than ordinary twins. It was possible that the closeness that existed in these cases was the result of a shared soul, while normal twins had their own separate identities, their spirits having arrived separately.

Much had been said on the ability of twins to communicate, that they shared a telepathic ability. He foraged in his mind to uncover what he could remember on this subject and he tried to communicate with the other baby but he always seemed to come up against a blank wall. He sensed that his sibling was too primitive or underdeveloped to open its mind to his probing and eventually he was forced by failure to give up these attempts. That was reasonable too, if his twin did not have the benefit of having retained its pre-life memory as he had, it would have to go through the whole tedious process of learning and growing up again.

His twin fascinated and abhorred him. Try as he might, he could not think of anything else. Even if he forgot about him for a moment, he would be suddenly reminded when receiving a kick or his brother's probing fingers touched his body unexpectedly.

He realised that time was running out in his cocoon but knew that there would be plenty of opportunity after his birth to worry about these things. He comforted himself with the thought that soon he would be able to see not only his twin, if it existed, but Judy as well. It wouldn't be very long before he would feel the comforting closeness of her skin as she held him secure in her arms. He conjured up an image of Judy and felt a great warmth sweep over him. Strangely the image that came to him was as much a maternal scene, as one having any sexual content. Her position in his mind was now a combination of mother and lover but as time passed the maternal influence seemed to be increasing subtly at the expense of his desire for her as a man. After all, he realised, he was no longer wholly a man, but a baby with a man's spirit. Any feelings he now had for her as a man were only those he had carried with him from his past life. In the picture he was presently seeing she was holding him lovingly to her breast and then she opened his little mouth with a finger. He saw himself enveloping her nipple in his tiny lips and sucking milk from her breasts and he could almost taste its sweetness.

The unborn foetus that was David Hawkin experienced its first tentative erection.

The realisation was comforting.

At least he now knew that he was still a male.

"Make sure she's asleep and the door is closed," whispered George.

Len opened the door carefully without making any undue noise. Then he stepped through to where the sedated form of Judy lay quietly asleep. After checking that she would not be easily disturbed by their movements next door, he returned to where George was standing before the panel of subdued lights on the console of equipment.

"Any idea what this lot's for guv?"

"No, but the terminal should give us the answers, it will all be controlled from there and one is much the same as another."

He didn't use the audio control but quickly worked his way into the system from the main menu until he found a directory labelled archive.

A sub menu displayed the different types of records held by the system including video. George requested VCR and was given a list showing the research program titles, dates and times. By finding the recordings made at the time of the deaths he retrieved the research program title, "RCARN."

"RCARN, doesn't mean sod all to me, how about you?" "Sorry Guv."

"Anyway, here goes...let's see what the buggers were

up to." He keyed in a request for a play back of the relevant recordings. The screen immediately flashed back a message.

'Access denied.'

'Who by?' He typed.

'Confidentiality request was submitted by Jonas Nichols and confirmed by the Chairman of the board of CDG.'

"We'll soon see about that."

Going back into the system he worked his way through the utilities until he came across what he was looking for, a staff directory for CDG. Right at the top was the CDG Chairman's internal telephone number, his mobile and to the DCI's satisfaction, his home number.

Oblivious of the time of day and the seniority of the man he was about to wake from his sleep, George picked up a phone and dialled the number. After a few moments a sleepy voice answered the phone.

"Good morning Mr Chapman. DCI Baxter, investigating the... er deaths at CDG laboratories. Sorry to bother you but I have a problem that you might be able to help me with."

He didn't sound sorry at all.

"Do you know what time it is?"

"Yes, of course I do. I wouldn't have called you if it wasn't important."

"Well what is it inspector? Now you have got me out of my bed I suppose you may as well go ahead and ask me whatever it is you think is so damned important that it can't wait until morning."

"I need access to certain computer recordings taken in Professor Hawkin's laboratory. I'm into the directory but my access has been barred and your name has cropped up."

"Yes, that's correct. Mr Nichols asked for my authorisation. Where exactly are you Inspector?"

"At your laboratories."

"My God man, who let you in? Is there anybody from my staff there?"

"No. I let myself in. Look I am not interested in whatever it is that they have been meddling with here. All I want is to see what happened at the time the men died. According to Nichols nothing was happening."

"Well, I.."

"This is a murder enquiry."

"Murder?"

"Beyond doubt. Look I nearly have everything I need, I just want this one little look at your records."

"I don't know....The project."

"I'm not interested in the project.......What about a compromise. Give me access to the recordings over a twenty minute period, ten before and ten after the deaths. You have my guarantee that anything I see or hear that is related to your project in any way at all, will be forgotten. I am a police inspector, you can trust me to be discreet."

The old man didn't answer straight away. Part of him thought he should tell this inspector to forget it, to come back to him in the morning. The other side just wanted to go back to bed and knew that the easiest way to achieve this was to give in to the request. After all, he asked himself, what harm can it do?

"If I agree, you will keep this entirely between ourselves?"

"You have my word," George smirked knowing he would get what he wanted and he added in the manner of an additional threat.

"Come on. I need this information and if I don't get it now, you know I will eventually."

"Yes, yes. Alright I'll make the arrangements in the morning."

"No, now! I wouldn't ask if I didn't need it. I'm sure you have a terminal in your home, it will only take you a moment."

"Oh...alright. Good night inspector."

"Good night, and...er thanks." George said grudgingly.

He heard the click as the line was disconnected.

George keyed in a new request and only had to wait a few minutes until the computer obtained the necessary clearance. Suddenly the screen blipped and scrolled a more detailed list of recordings and times. George scanned through to make sure the equipment had been active during the period when the two men had died.

"Look there Len," he whispered, poking a finger at the screen.

"It looks like we're in luck."

George hurriedly keyed in more instructions and suddenly the digital recording appeared on the computer screen. Both men watched with mounting excitement.

They saw the drinks being brought in by Michael and heard the toast to the Professor.

"This is it Len!"

Almost immediately they saw the professor and the woman slump to the floor. The efforts that Michael Tamasoto made to stay on his feet impressed them but most noticeable were Jonas's actions. As the others collapsed he stood there and watched. From what you could see of his features there didn't seem to be too much surprise registered there. Then Jonas rushed to attend to David and the woman and they saw him struggle to lift her unconscious form onto the beds. Just as he turned and walked back across the room the recording went blank.

George keyed in a request.

'No more data available,' came the reply on the screen.

"Shit, the bastard wiped it!" Exclaimed George.

He thought about this for a moment then decided to run through what they had seen again. In fact, at George's insistence, they reviewed the ten minutes or so of recording several more times, sometimes freezing a scene and frequently rewinding a section to give particular attention to one scene or other. Len was soon bored and feeling very tired but knew better than to show it. Between suppressed yawns he managed to seem attentive for fear of George's reaction. George on the other hand was devoting one hundred per cent attention to the recordings. He took a pad and pencil and started to jot down notes, highlighting particular points that he wished to refer back to later. It was not until he was satisfied that he hadn't missed anything that he relaxed and turned on Len once more.

"Ok, what have we got here?"

Trying very hard to show an interest Len rubbed his eyes and summoned his thoughts.

"They were all there; Tamasoto brought out the drinks." "What else?"

"That's enough isn't it. It was the drinks that were poisoned."

"Crap!" Said George who enjoyed using Len's limited intellect as a sounding post. He was fully aware that his assistant wasn't the brightest person in the world and knew that he would undoubtedly jump to those wrong conclusions.

He also enjoyed showing his assistant how clever he was.

"Did you see the expression on Nichols's face when the others started collapsing? No surprise there at all. Then what did he do? He dragged the professor and the girl onto the beds but he didn't even look at Tamasoto. The guy could have evaporated for all he cared."

"Yeah! You're right."

"Of course I'm right. Did you see what the professor had in his hands when he collapsed?"

"The er..glass?"

"What else?"

"I don't know guv, nothing. I don't think he had anything else in his hands."

"That's right Len. That's the point I'm making. He wasn't holding anything else at all.....but when we got here we found a syringe in his right hand. So where did that appear from?"

"The pathologist's report said he could have injected himself after he collapsed, but he didn't have the syringe."

"So Nichols must have stuck the needle in the professor's arm then put the syringe in his hand after he put him on the bed. It's my bet that Nichols killed them and its all got something to do with their work. That's where we will find a motive," he stopped speaking and gave the whole thing a bit more thought. Why were they toasting the professor? He asked himself, He hadn't got much to laugh about by the look of him. Was he going somewhere?

STILLBORN

"I know it's him. Knew it from the minute I set eyes on him and now this lot takes us part way there. All we need to know now is exactly what they were up to, we have to find out about their work."

Len yawned, unable to control himself any longer.

"Look guv we've got everything that we can from here. Its gone five o'clock, why don't we pack it in until tomorrow?"

But George was the exact opposite of his assistant. He felt wide awake. His adrenaline was flowing like a hunter ready to pounce on its victim and knowing the identity of his prey only increased his desire to pursue this through to the end.

"Take a few hours off Len. Make sure you're back here before eight."

"Thanks guv. What about you?"

"Oh I'll just sit here a while. I've got some thinking to do."

George leaned back and closed his eyes in thought. Len was glad of the unexpected dismissal and didn't waste any time leaving in case George changed his mind. He moved quickly to the door and made his way out of the complex.

Once he was alone George played the recordings again and carefully went over every detail, stopping regularly to make more notes. He thought about the girl. What had he missed? There was something nagging in his brain and it was to do with her. He went over in his mind the last time that he had questioned Jonas and found himself going carefully over why she was still in the laboratory and not in a clinic or at home. Her baby was due any day and if she didn't leave soon she'd end up having it here, in the laboratory. Why is she still here? He asked himself. She'll have the baby here.

That's it! He slammed his fist down on the desk.

That's what they want. She's part of it all, her, the baby, they're all part of whatever it is that's going on here.

He stopped the recording and went through to where Judy was sleeping. Without putting on the lights he placed his hand over her mouth and held her there while her startled eyes flickered open. Seeing him looming over her they widened in horror.

"You and me are going to have a little chat lady."

He wanted to scare her, frighten her to the point where her resistance would crumble and she would tell him what he wanted to know. It had to be done quickly, decisively, while she was still in the uncertain nether region between dreams and wakefulness. Before the psychological barriers could slide into place and harden her resolve.

Keeping his hand held tight over her mouth he asked his question while looking deep into her eyes.

"Why are you still here in the laboratory?" He slowly took his hand away and waited for her choked reply.

"I can't..." She spluttered.

Tears ran down her cheeks and she was hardly able to talk between sobs. Without a second thought he slapped her hard across her face with the back of his hand. It was enough. Fear of this man overcame her fear of Jonas Nichols.

"The transfer....," she sobbed. "David is in here..."

She jabbed a shaking hand towards her belly.

"What the fuck are you talking about girl? Start from the beginning...and slowly!"

She tried hard to control her breathing, to stop the sobs that racked her body and interfered with her speech. She told him everything she knew and he sat quietly listening to what she was saying, not daring to interrupt in case it caused her to hesitate and lose her train of thought. She told him much more than he had expected to hear. Not only about the transfer and David's work but also of her confusion and her feelings for Michael and such was the sadness with which she described him that even George was not unaffected. Perhaps once, long ago, he had loved somebody in the same way and had also lost them and perhaps his own loss had caused him to build up this wall of hardness around his heart that people saw in him.

Eventually the story was told and Judy's words faltered and having told him all she knew she collapsed into her own misery once again. George sat quietly beside her, his strong arm around her shoulder, his gruff policeman's face gone, being replaced by one that was almost human. He took a tissue from the cabinet beside her bed and wiped her face gently before saying in a quiet voice.

"You don't have to worry. There won't be any repercussions against you. I have my answers now and the fish I am about to fry will be enough."

"Thank you...... ," she sobbed.

"Do you know, I'm glad you made me tell you," her bottom lip quivered as if she was about to cry again but a tentative smile formed about her eyes.

"I hope you find out what happened. There's ....there's only one thing I regret now," She lay back and closed her eyes before continuing.

"I wish it was Michael who was living inside me and not David."

Not many people saw this side of George, the man

210

behind the mask. Certainly he was hard, sometimes almost cruel. He was also fair and served justice well. He leaned over and kissed her gently on the forehead, a final token of thanks, not for the information she had given him but for the fleeting memories she had stirred. She wouldn't see him like this again and she knew it. She watched him as he turned and walked out of the room and her last thought as he disappeared was that he was a little like Michael. At the door he turned one last time.

"I'm sorry about Tamasoto...Michael. He must have been OK."

George walked quietly back to David's office and sat down. Suddenly he felt drained, exhausted by the unexpected release of his own emotions as much as by the fact it was already morning. At the same time he felt satisfied that he had got to the bottom of this little intrigue. He dropped down on to the couch, stretching out on his back and considered all she had told him. He closed his eyes and let the mental images act out the scenes she had described and in a very short space of time he had drifted off into a sleep where those same re-enactments became distorted in his dreams.

In the room down the corridor Judy also drifted off into a fitful sleep. Her dreams became nightmares, all the recent pain came back, perhaps stimulated by what was happening inside her. The stress of what she had just endured had caused unexpected amounts of chemicals to flow through her body and these in turn caused other things to happen within her system that pre-empted the natural conclusion of her pregnancy. As the first minute contractions occurred,

STILLBORN

Judy tossed uncomfortably in her sleep and saw visions of her baby in many unearthly forms. Each time the distorted image had David's face grinning inanely at her, that toothless mouth would open as if to utter cries of contemptuous triumph and she would cry out and see the hazy image of somebody trying to reach her through a tangled web with mists that fell and hid him from her view. Then as that ethereal being fought its way towards her she would suddenly see this other face loom up, pain etched in its features which were those of Michael. As she reached out to him his face would dissolve and become the harder outlines of George Baxter. The figure grew close then staggered and fell, hands outstretched towards her. She struggled to reach out and touch those fingers but the thing that was half in and half out of her belly would grin and pull her back. In the mists behind this image she would see another man approach, a huge bloated figure, a caricature of Jonas and in its hand was a huge curved knife.

As the desperate figure of Michael stretched and reached towards her, Jonas would plunge the knife repeatedly in his back, each time lifting the blade high in the mist so that it glinted as some hidden light illuminated its blade. She could see the blood, brilliant red and frothing, drip from its tip. Each time the muscles in her belly contracted, the blade would pierce Michael's back and the skin around his mouth would stretch tight in a scream.

She awoke suddenly and the images faded, lost forever in some remote corner of her mind. As the dream died and the ugly reality of the present returned, the pain racked vision of Michael slowly wavered and transcended into the gentle features of the doctor who was leaning over her, his hand gently pressed against her shoulder.

"Are you alright Judy?"

"Yes. Yes thank you doctor. Everything will be alright now."

"Good. Just call if you need me, I'll only be next door."

"Thank you doctor."

As he turned to leave, she reached out and took his hand.

"Doctor, I think it is starting."

Some distance away in his comfortable apartment, Jonas was preparing himself for the day ahead.

He had slept well, waking to the sound of his alarm he had struggled to hang on to the memory of his dreams in which he stood out god-like, surrounded by the diminutive figures of all the normal people who were mere mortals. The dreams that his disturbed self conscious created were ones of self adulation, narcissistic and full of self gratification.

He had woken with a self satisfied expression on his face and as he eked out the last enjoyable memories of his dreams and replaced those memories with anticipation for the day ahead, he had no sense of foreboding for what was about to occur.

The phone rang and he quickly recognised the slightly worried voice of Judy's doctor.

"Good morning doctor. What can I do for you?"

"Judy has just started her labour. I think it will be quite some time yet but I thought I should let you know."

"That's just fine doctor. I'll be there as soon as possible."

STILLBORN

Jonas put the phone down and rubbed his hands together in anticipation. Finally, he thought, it's going to happen.

He hurried as he completed his preparations for the day ahead and was soon on his way to the laboratory. Any passer-by would have noticed the bounce in his step and the smile on his face as he hurried forward to greet his destiny.

CHAPTER FIFTEEN

The contractions were now occurring every ten minutes or so and causing David more distress than he had anticipated. The muscular convulsions were slowly thrusting him downwards, behind and towards his twin. Sometimes he could feel those little feet touch his head as his brother also struggled against the inevitable.

Increasingly he was paying more attention to his twin and it was definitely not only on a physical level. He also seemed to be building up a mental or spiritual link and he had the uncomfortable feeling that he knew his brother in some way from his previous life. At the same time he was annoyed that while having this awareness of familiarity, he couldn't quite place him. Many times he tried again to make some kind of telepathic communication but the responses and images he received frightened him, not because of their clarity but their content. Rather than feel that he had established communication at a linguistic level, he received images, not detailed pictures of people or places, but images that seemed to represent basic characteristics of behaviour and feeling. He realised that his twin would not have the benefit of memory and therefore appreciated that the thought patterns that he was receiving could only exist at this kind of level.

All the same he was intimidated.

Worst of all was the aggression he felt. Far from brotherly love, he was picking up feelings of independence that bordered on hostility, as if his brother was already vying for his mother's affection.

STILLBORN

In contrast to this aggression he also recognised a level of fraternity, a physical bonding that established their roles as brothers while at the same time the messages he was receiving certainly said, 'Yes, you are my brother, we do share that much, but I will try to take everything before you can reach it, every morsel of food, every drop of our mothers milk will only be surrendered to you by force.'

It seemed so strange to him that a foetal child could have such powerful emotions, feelings that bordered on hate.

Of course David had no idea that his sibling may also know him, that from his perspective David's presence here had engendered these feelings, that he was as much an unwanted intrusion to his brother, as his brother was to him.

The feelings frightened him, he tried to close them out but still his little frame shuddered at the idea even though he still bathed in the warmth and security of his mothers bodily fluids.

Quickly, he changed the direction of his telepathic efforts and tried to link his mind with that of Judy. He tried to reach her with thoughts of love but felt a wall of rejection close around her mind, a dark cold wall that prevented him from reaching inside. At the same time he felt the slow development of a kind of love from her at what he would call a chemical level and he considered this the beginnings of their bonding process.

It was some time now since he had slept for more than a few minutes. Each time he drifted off he would be suddenly awakened by the next set of contractions. Feelings of tiredness washed over him as he was subjected to the pressure of contracting muscles around his body. When they were particularly severe he would experience moments of panic as his pulse fluttered in response to the trauma.

He wondered how Judy was feeling at this moment. Not as bad as he did, he guessed. She certainly wouldn't be experiencing any pain because she would be protected by her epidural, but at the same time he was sure she would be sharing this overwhelming tiredness.

The contractions subsided once again and almost immediately David slipped into a brief and fitful sleep.

Judy relaxed again as her body returned to normal. She looked around and noticed the doctor busying himself at a desk and was aware of Jonas coming into the room. She didn't return the smile he gave her, his presence rekindled the feelings of hate she was building against him and how she blamed him for who was in her womb. She gritted her teeth, not against any pain, but almost in defiance of the creature she was about to give birth to. Turning her face away from the direction of Jonas she closed her eyes and tried to control her breathing as the next set of contractions began. She listened to the conversation between the doctor and Jonas with more interest than she appeared to be taking.

"How is your patient doctor?"

"She's fine Mr Nichols, well into the final stages now. The birth should take place within the hour. Will you er......be present?"

"Yes, of course, I.."

"No!" Yelled Judy taking a sudden and somewhat violent interest. "I don't want him here. Is that clear!"

217

STILLBORN

She turned her head towards him with such a cold look in her eyes that even Jonas was taken aback.

"Judy my dear. Aren't you forgetting how much effort we have put in to creating this moment?"

"You didn't!" She spat. "Michael and David did all the work. You just want the credit."

His face coloured; at first with embarrassment, then with anger.

"Now listen to me. If it wasn't for my intervention you would be in very serious trouble with the police by now."

"Bullshit! There is absolutely no way you are going to be present at the birth of my child."

"Alright Judy, just calm down," interrupted the doctor turning towards Jonas who was glowering at the girl on the bed, unable to repress his anger.

"I'm sorry Mr Nichols. As Judy's doctor I must see that her wishes are respected. If she doesn't want you here that is her right."

Judy smiled triumphantly at Jonas. She saw the diplomatic smile on his face disappear and felt a shiver run through her as it was replaced with a sneer. Enraged Jonas turned to leave.

"You'll regret this,"

"Oh, by the way Mr Nichols," added the doctor almost as an afterthought, "That police inspector is waiting in your office. He told me to tell you in case you came here first."

"In my office....," Jonas' step faltered and he turned to look at the doctor but said nothing. He was far too angry. He just gave Judy one more derisory glare then marched out of the room.

"Damn!", he muttered to himself. "And today of all days." He marched down the corridor towards his

office and was surprised to find George Baxter's
assistant draped insolently over a chair in his
reception area, his head buried in a magazine.

"I heard Baxter wanted to see me?"

"Yeah that's right. He's waiting inside," Len's reply
was casual, he didn't even bother to look up, "I'd get
in there quick if I were you, he's been waiting a while.
Doesn't like people to keep him waiting."

"Who do you think you're talking to and who the hell
does he think he is helping himself to my office?"

Len didn't even answer. He just carried on reading
his magazine and ignored him. Jonas was left there,
standing open mouthed and boiling over in fury. Lost
for words Jonas strode past Len and into his office
where, to even more amazement, he found George
Baxter sitting in his chair with his feet on the desk.
George was leaning back supporting his head in his
hands and to all intents appeared to be asleep.

"Sit." Commanded George without even moving..

"Now look here..."

George looked at him then, his eyes as cold as
diamonds. A little, cruel smile played around the
corners of his mouth.

"No! This time you listen. I'm conducting a murder
investigation and I want some answers and this time
you are going to give them to me."

Again Jonas was about to protest but before he could
utter a word George walked around the desk and
pushed Jonas into a chair. Then he returned to
Jonas's huge leather swivel chair, leaned back and
rubbed his bloodshot eyes. When he spoke again it
was quietly but barely concealed disgust was in his
voice as well as his expression.

"Now tell me why you killed Michael Tamasoto?"

STILLBORN

Jonas began to feel scared.

Suddenly the protection of the amniotic fluid disappeared and the walls of flesh collapsed around him, the uterine muscles forcing the liquid out like air from a burst tyre.

The feeling was awful. One minute he was lying safe and warm then suddenly the whole world seemed to close in around him and he experienced the heart wrenching fear of a claustrophobic trapped in the tiniest of spaces. Judy's flesh enveloped him like cling-film and when contractions were occurring he could feel the pressure of her muscles in a much more direct way than before, as if he was held in a giant hand covered in oil that squeezed, and in so doing, forced him to slide ever downwards towards the waiting world.

Expecting to be thrust out into the open at any second he prepared himself for the final terrifying journey into the world. Then just as quickly as the contractions had started so too they suddenly stopped and he was left trapped like a chrysalis within this cocoon of flesh.

Slowly he drew on his mental reserves and forcibly calmed himself through a series of mental incantations. At the same time he tried hard to ignore the now wild fluctuations of his heartbeat that seemed one moment to be beating at supersonic speed and the next stopping for such long periods that he felt himself drifting towards unconsciousness. He was also aware of more movement from his mother who seemed to be reacting to the strain of labour quite violently. It was difficult to estimate her position except in relation to his own but at least he knew that he was correctly positioned for birth.

He realised that they were now undergoing the final stages of their birth and from his own position he knew that his brother would be born first. If he could have chosen he would certainly have gone before him and he just hoped that there would not be too much of a delay between their births because the distress he was feeling was becoming unbearable. Suddenly they came again, stronger than ever. Beneath him his brother shot away into the outside world and David felt his little body pushed through the pelvis. As this happened the pressure on his brain intensified as the sections of bone were compressed.

Like an old and frightened man, David tried vainly to utter a scream. His trembling lips curled back and the exposed gums turned purple through lack of oxygen.

Held vice like, he was unable to move, to escape the agony of this moment.

Vague shadows deepened in colour, contrasting with the flashes of brilliant light that accompanied the fiercest of pains. David hid in the temporary refuge of oblivion.

Although she felt no pain, Judy's face was drenched in sweat from the sheer muscular effort that child-birth required. It had not been a particularly long labour and the pain had been eliminated by the use of a spinal anaesthetic.

The experience was having an effect on the way Judy felt, the closer she came to giving birth, the more she felt a desire to hold this unknown offspring in her arms.

Mother-Nature was overriding her intellectual fears.

STILLBORN

When labour first began she had felt relief. Relief that this baby whom she had come to hate, the child of her dreams with David's grinning features, would finally be expunged from her body. She hadn't given the outcome much consideration except that she was firm in the resolve that she could not rear this child that contained David's spirit. She felt that because of this intrusion, David had somehow deprived her of a future with the man she now loved. But determined as she was, and even after considering all the nightmares that she had lived through, her body chemistry had begun to make subtle changes to the way in which she was viewing her unborn child.

So it was that as her labour progressed her thoughts of ridding herself of this unwanted intruder were slowly replaced with new feelings dictated by the needs that motherhood imposed on her. She thought less about who was inside her baby's body, her mind seemed to be filling with the desire to produce and nurture a living being but even so she still felt that when the child was born and she recognised her baby for who it was, she would lose any maternal desire to foster it.

For the time being at least, she was totally absorbed with the birth itself and as the moment approached that surreptitious desire to hold her baby in her arms increased.

"You are nearly there Judy. I can see the top of the head. Next time the contractions start I want you to really try and push downwards," the midwife instructed her.

Judy breathed rhythmically, summoning her strength for the next and hopefully, the final effort. The doctor wiped her face with a cool scented tissue and she felt rather than saw the two nurses hovering around her lower body.

"Thanks. I'll try," she looked into the kind face of the doctor who stood beside her. He had been there constantly for the past hour or so. She was grateful to him for having saved her from Jonas' presence at the birth. Even now as she remembered his greedy eyes scanning her body as he announced that he would be there, she gave an involuntary shudder. Slowly her breathing relaxed until just as it was approaching its normal pace and depth, she felt the next contraction begin.

Waiting, drawing on her resources, she anticipated the moment when the spasm would be at its peak. As that point approached she released all her will and strength in one enormous effort to push the child from within her. Even through the blank wall that the anaesthetic had built around her nerve endings, she flinched as she felt the sinews stretching and the skin tear.

Then just as she was about to give that final push the contraction just as quickly subsided. She looked up into the doctor's eyes and became aware of how tightly she was gripping his hand and even though she was unhappy about her situation she could not help the feeling of wonder at what was happening to her, sharing the moment that millions of women through time immemorial had also experienced. The unique and incomparable joy of motherhood began to fill her being and tears of a kind of joy sprang from her eyes.

"That's great Judy, the head is out. Next time just one final effort and it will all be over."

She heard the subdued voices of the nurses as they

busied themselves and heard plopping sounds as they gently used small suction tubes to clear the mucus from her baby's face. She didn't have time to speak before she was gritting her teeth in that final effort to release the child from within her.

Then it was over.

Her child was born, she heard its cry and felt a shiver run through her body. The midwife tried to put the baby on her chest but she closed her eyes and turned her head sideways, her raised hand denying acceptance of her child.

"It's OK Judy. We will bring him back later. Nurse take the baby away."

She turned quickly and took the baby over to a bench where she attended to its needs, dressing the severed cord, washing and cleaning its frail body.

Judy lay her head back and felt her muscles relax, first in her face and neck, then those in her shoulders and arms. She slowly relaxed her intense grip on the doctor's hand and felt him gently wipe away the sweat from her forehead.

"Congratulations Judy. You have a healthy baby boy."

She heaved a sigh of relief and felt a profound sense of achievement and was somewhat delirious from the effort, the drugs or perhaps unexpectedly, from the mere accomplishment of having produced a healthy baby boy. Her eyes opened and she gazed into the doctor's face. He saw the sparkle there and as always was engulfed by the magic of this moment. Then he saw that joy fade and slip away as Judy came back to reality, as the pressures of childbirth and the maternal euphoria were swept away by the returning image deep in her mind of that baby boy, and who or what it was.

She briefly imagined it being handed to her and of her holding the bundle close and using a finger to gingerly pull the blankets to expose its face and of the sudden horror as a lined and wizened version of David's features opened its mouth in a toothless grin. In a desperate effort to quell the nightmare within her she closed her eyes and concentrated her thoughts on her memory of Michael's warm and loving face. The doctor saw her expression change and was filled with the sadness that he sensed in Judy. In an innocent attempt to sustain her spirits he quietly said.

"They will bring your baby back very soon Judy. Then you can hold him in your arms."

"No! I don't want it near me."

The doctor said nothing in reply, not understanding the reasons that drove her to despise her new born child.

In the background Judy could hear the plaintive cry of her baby. The sounds just about touched her consciousness before she blotted them out. Even so she felt goose pimples on her skin and she was filled with that cold air of anticipation. Judy ignored the cries, refused to recognise something familiar in the sounds her baby made.

STILLBORN

CHAPTER SIXTEEN

"You must see your baby," the doctor said gently. "Its very important for both of you that bonding starts as soon as possible."

"I'm sorry doctor, I just can't. I....you wouldn't understand." She felt quite calm now as long as he was there. She had grown to trust the doctor who seemed to be very kind and understanding. She gave him a little smile and repeated mournfully. "You wouldn't understand."

"Try me," he said gently taking her hand. "In my job I've heard most things. You won't shock me and it may help just to talk about it with someone else, somebody who isn't directly involved."

"I don't know if I should...he told me not to talk to anyone else about it."

"Who..the police inspector?"

"No. Jonas Nichols."

"He won't know what we talk about. You know that I can't tell anyone else, its against my oath as a doctor and..."

"Yes?", she said tentatively, almost eagerly.

"Well we've come to know each other quite well. I.... well I like you Judy. You have my word as a man as well as your doctor that this will be between you and me."

"Yes. I know," she squeezed his hand gratefully and closed her eyes. She trusted him and perhaps it would help to get it off her chest she decided. "I'll tell you."

Over the next few minutes she told him everything, surprised at herself in the way she was able to tell him of her feelings. He didn't interrupt her and she did not see any censure or criticism in his eyes. He just listened attentively, occasionally smiling or patting her hand reassuringly when she hesitated.

Eventually she had said it all, told him everything that had happened and all that she felt. She lay back with her eyes closed and waited for him to respond but he did not say anything immediately. He gave the whole matter a lot of thought before speaking and when he did it was in a reassuring voice that only helped her to relax even more.

"You must see the baby Judy..... it may hurt, but do it now. Just to know for certain. After all, the reality won't be as bad as your dreams and just seeing him may help to dispel those nightmares," he paused before continuing as if to give her time to let the words sink in.

"You will always wonder if you don't see for yourself. You will always carry feelings of guilt and regret."

She didn't answer straight away. His words had certainly only reinforced her basic maternal desire to see her child, a feeling that now almost overwhelmed her other fears.

"This is a terrible mess," she sobbed. "I've got a healthy baby boy. I don't know who is the natural father, David or Michael. I also don't know who is inside my baby's head, one of them, none of them, I don't know. Michael said he would take care of things, perhaps he did. I...I just don't know what to do."

He put an arm around her heaving shoulders and held her like that until her tears subsided.

"Even if you are right and the transfer happened, the implications are probably nothing like you have been imagining. I've delivered hundreds of babies and I've yet to see a normal healthy baby that disgusts me. A baby is an empty vessel, life makes it into the person it becomes."

"Exactly! Except in my case my baby will already have had a lifetime's experiences, including...."

"Come on Judy, let's hear it?"

"Well. He...David has slept with me.......my own baby will have intimate knowledge of me..."

"Yes, I see. Okay, what if it is Michael in there?" He noticed her face light up, a smile of hope form around her eyes. "It could be you know, they were both in the room."

"Yes."

"From what you have told me he would also have..intimate knowledge of you."

"Yes but don't you see, he didn't have the drug, he won't remember," her hand clasped his in her excitement. "Oh if it is Michael's spirit that would be perfect. I know my baby would be kind, gentle...all those good things........if Michael is in there I don't think I would ever tell him. That would be the difference - he wouldn't know!"

"Well it seems that is a chance you are going to have to take. If you don't you will never know if you rejected the wrong baby."

She sighed and opened her eyes to look into his. Her emotions were at war, her feelings in confusion but suddenly she decided to do as he said.

"Alright doctor, I'll do it."

"Good. I'll go and get him straight away."

"No...not yet."

"Yes Judy. Do it now or you may put it off for ever."

She knew that what he was saying was right but she was still terribly afraid of facing what may be a realisation of her nightmares.

"Yes you're right. I'll see him," she said with resignation. With a sigh of relief he got up and walked out of the room. Judy's heart was pounding uncontrollably and she did her best to repress the sudden images that came to her from her nightmares. She forced her eyes wide open and pinched herself to stop her mind wandering. She started to count the twinkling lights on the medical display panel like an insomniac counting sheep. But in her case it was to avoid the return of the frightening images that came with sleep.

The interrogation was going badly for Jonas.

Being the sort of self-righteous man that he was, the attack that George Baxter had launched was difficult for him to withstand. He wasn't used to having his actions questioned and even when he had to persuade others to change their views, he used attacking rather than defensive tactics. It wasn't working with the inspector, Jonas didn't know how to ward off the barrage of insults, accusations and innuendos.

At first he tried to bluster his way through, answering the accusations with contemptuous replies. It didn't work. George was not going to let go now that he had his teeth into the matter.

"Why did you kill Michael Tamasoto?"

Jonas huffed and puffed, his face red and swollen. He lifted himself up to his full height and tried to reply with an air of authority.

"Don't be ridiculous," he said dismissively. "And get your feet off my desk."

The policeman did. Standing up slowly he advanced on the big man with menace in his eyes and reaching out a hand pushed Jonas down into his seat.

"You nearly got away with it, the suicide note was a good touch, almost had me convinced....but there's no escape. I know you did it, I've seen the tapes," he paused to watch Jonas's reaction, saw the eyelids flutter, the tongue come out to moisten the lips.

"There's no way out of this so are you going to make this easy or do we have to do it the hard way? Why did you kill Tamasoto?"

George stayed where he was, leaning over Jonas threateningly. Jonas still tried desperately to retrieve control of the situation but he was floundering badly.

"If you don't get out of my office immediately!" He yelled. "You will regret it. I have a lot of influential friends. In the very near future I could be taking a seat on the board of CDG. Inspector, if you care about your own position I would think seriously about adopting a different attitude."

Jonas was shaking as he spoke, partly from fear but mostly from anger.

George laughed out loud then jabbed a finger into Jonas' chest.

"I know about the transfer. I know where the professor is right at this moment."

The bombshell dropped just as he had intended it to. Jonas was unable to speak, his bloated features quickly took on a new aspect, changing rapidly from deep red to ash grey. The shaking increased but was now from fear rather than anger. Even the fleshy jowls of his face shook uncontrollably.

"You...you know?" He asked weakly.

"Yes Nichols, I know. Now you tell me why you killed Tamasoto? I don't know whether or not you killed the professor but I do know you killed Tamasoto. So why? Was he an inconvenience? Did he stand in your way somehow, a threat to your own crazy desire for power? Come on, answer me you bastard!"

Jonas's huge frame seemed to shrink as he collapsed inwardly. All defiance was gone and he could now only think of his own survival. Like a trapped and wounded animal he quickly shifted the emphasis of his emotions from anger to cunning. If it was required he would grovel but for the time being at least he would try to turn this around.

"Alright! I'll tell you. I did know that the professor was about to take his own life, he was dying anyway and he thought that by doing so he could assist the research and perhaps achieve some sort of immortality for himself."

Jonas wiped his forehead nervously and paused for breath before continuing. The inspector turned away prepared to listen to the man's lies, knowing that eventually he would trap himself. He walked over to Jonas's chair behind the large desk and slid down into a relaxed position, his hands meeting across his stomach. Jonas did not object this time but having restored a little self confidence continued with his answer.

"I covered up for him. The research was extremely important so I went along with his proposal. Yes I know, perhaps I shouldn't have, but surely you can see why?" Jonas looked at George with a mixture of hope and pleading in his eyes but failing to obtain any response he continued.

"Then I found out that Michael was having an affair with Judy, the woman that David loved. Now doesn't it seem logical that David decided to kill him, he had nothing to lose, he couldn't even be brought to book for that one."

Jonas stopped speaking and breathed deeply. George said nothing immediately and Jonas mistakenly interpreted this as the policeman's acceptance of what he had said. He began to relax slightly but was brought back to reality with a jolt.

"No, it doesn't wash Nichols," George stated in a smooth and controlled tone.

"It's good but not quite good enough. First of all it was very unlikely that the Professor knew of the relationship between Judy and Tamasoto.."

"But we can't be certain, can we?" Interjected Jonas in desperation.

George ignored this and continued, marking off the points as he went with the index finger of his right hand against the palm of the other.

"Secondly. Wouldn't you agree that the professor was a logical man, a scientist of the highest calibre. A genius I think you said?"

"Yes," agreed Jonas weakly. "But..."

"And the professor had prepared the transfer right down to the last detail. With his own future at stake he wouldn't have taken a chance on the outcome by some stupid, emotional course of action. Would he?"

"No, but..."

George held up his hand to silence him.

"So by killing Tamasoto at the same time that he took his own life he would be going against everything he believed in. Who was going to ensure the transfer was carried out according to plan? There was nobody else present, no other technician briefed to take over in the case of an emergency," he paused and looked into the man's face and saw the control going again. Jonas was losing focus, a myriad of twinkling lights danced in eyes brimming over with fear as if he was drowning.

"By killing Michael he was certainly jeopardizing the outcome of the transfer of his own spirit. He would have been committing suicide in more ways than one, spiritually as well as physically. How was he to know what would have happened when by killing Tamasoto he was releasing a second spirit in the chamber? Tamasoto's spirit may have taken his place in the unborn child."

George saw the shock of realisation spread over Jonas's features.

"The professor wouldn't make that kind of mistake. You might."

Jonas gasped as the thought struck home. He had allowed this to happen and now he was losing everything. He didn't even know if the transfer had been a success. He hadn't even checked on Tamasoto or given the matter of his death a second thought.

His thoughts went back to the transfer itself, there had been that flash. He hadn't actually seen David's spirit enter the body of the pregnant woman. He cursed himself, how could he have been that stupid? Suddenly he felt his will disintegrate into a thousand parts as he realised that he had failed. He wanted desperately to deny what was happening, what was being said but he could only open and shut his mouth like a fish out of water and no sound came, no voice of denial. Vaguely he could hear George Baxter continuing his litany of proof against him but he could do nothing to defend himself.

"...and you seemed fully prepared to take over. A bit unusual that isn't it? That you should be so fully conversant with the processes involved. After all, that wouldn't normally be within your field of responsibility. You are an administrator not a scientist, isn't that so Jonas? That's the third point."

Again he stopped to watch Jonas squirming in his seat, the sweat now running down his ashen cheeks and the fat jowls shaking like jelly. He laughed out loud again, enjoying the moment, sensing the man's breaking point was approaching. He did not let up, did not give him the chance to recover. George got out of his seat and walked around to the same side of the desk as Jonas and sitting on the corner, wagged a finger in his direction as he continued.

"Number four, and certainly the most damaging to you Nichols. The tape had been wiped. Now who apart from you had that sort of access. I checked that you were the only one who could do this. I checked the log and guess what? The computer filed your access the night you meddled with the tapes. Just you, nobody else chum."

Jonas felt as if he was dying, he was having difficulty breathing and he gasped out his interruption,

"Please...please, no more.."

"Oh yes, there's more, "continued George almost sadistically relishing Jonas's distress and revelling in his own moment of triumph as he watched this arrogant man wilt before him.

"Fifth point," he spat out sarcastically.

"No...No more."

But George would not be denied.

"Fifth point. You left enough on the tape to incriminate yourself. When the professor took the drug or as we both know, when you gave it to him, there was no syringe in his hand," he leant forward so that his face was only inches from Jonas's. "But when we found him it was in his hand. Now who put it there, there were only the four of you and the other three were in no condition to do anything."

George's eyes were sparkling. He was really pleased with himself and the effect his words were having on Jonas and it was probably because of his feeling of self satisfaction and confidence that he was just a little bit too relaxed. He was taken by complete surprise when Jonas reacted as he did. Jonas' world exploded.

There was nothing left, no future, no dreams. All his plans had crumbled, he wouldn't be the saviour of mankind, he wouldn't be chairman of the board of CDG as he deserved. Because of this ignorant, sadistic creature grinning at him, he had lost everything.

The world became distorted as the anger built within him.

DCI George Baxter, the object of his hate, took on absurd proportions through the sweat and tears that stung his eyes. He lunged forward with surprising speed and clamped his hands around George's throat before he could even cry out.

"You bastard!" Jonas screamed. "Just like the rest of them. Who cares about Tamasoto, a fucking foreigner!"

George's hands automatically grasped Jonas's wrists but he was no match for his sheer size and weight. He used all his strength in an effort to free himself but already he felt blackness descending upon him as they crashed onto the floor. He kicked out desperately feeling his boots scraping Jonas's shin. He lunged forward and his forehead crashed into

STILLBORN

Jonas's nose, he felt the cartilage give way but still there was no escape, Jonas's mind was now impervious to the rationality of pain. He could feel his strength slipping away and in desperation he released his hands from Jonas's wrists, clawed desperately at his face, feeling the skin tear and the blood dampen his fingers.

Just before losing his vision completely he could see Jonas's bulging hate filled eyes grinning insanely at him. He felt saliva, blood, sweat and tears drip onto his face and was aware of the vomit rising in his throat.

Then blackness.

The sun shone brightly on the Californian playing field. The captain of the home team ran ahead of the pack. Sweat drenched his tunic and the sinews in his face stood out reflecting the effort that he was putting into the game. He turned on his heels and looked back to see the ball spiralling towards him, momentarily blocking the sun's rays that enshrouded the ball with its brilliance. Even as he skidded to a stop he jumped to reach the ball. Muscles in his legs bulged from the effort and his shoulders felt as if red hot needles ran through them. The ball touched his fingertips and he drew it towards his body as he dropped back down towards the ground.

Still twisting, still falling, he didn't see the other team's defence until it was too late. Suddenly they were upon him. He sensed rather than felt the tackle from behind and threw himself forward towards the line. They came down on him heavily, his body twisted at an awkward angle, ball tucked close to his body, held there by his left hand as his right pushed out, trying to avoid the tackle. The sound of bones splintering was audible, air gushed from his lungs, silence fell over the stadium. The pack cleared except for Michael. His body was twisted, his back bent at an unnatural angle over the ball, his face wreathed in agony.

The image faded as she saw the doctor walking slowly towards her holding the small covered bundle in his arms that was her baby. Michael's face dissolved, the agony on the suntanned features replaced by the doctor's smile.

She felt as if she wanted to leap out of bed and run as fast as she could away from this nightmare, away from what she knew she had to do. She knew he was beside the bed and much against her will she forced herself to turn her head and look at him. It seemed as if everything was happening in slow motion and when she saw him lower the bundle into her arms it was as if on film, as if it was happening to somebody else. Then it was there, the weight of the baby resting heavily in her arms. Very slowly she looked down to see the child. It was covered with the blanket, a fold of which had fallen across its face. She remembered her last nightmare when she had uncovered David's grinning features.

Very gently, almost tentatively, her hand went down to the bundle and with one finger she drew back the blanket. Her breathing had stopped momentarily and the only thing that made her go on was the need to release herself from this spell and take in more air. She felt light headed, almost on the point of fainting. She slowly drew back the blanket, first uncovering its tiny pink forehead, then its eyes and eventually the whole face.

STILLBORN

Still she did not see its features, her mind refusing to let her eyes focus on what was in front of her. Then slowly, through the tears, the shape of the face appeared to take on form until at last she was seeing her baby clearly. She couldn't move, her gaze held spellbound as she saw him for the first time. This was her child.

And his!

The doctor was watching her with concern and as she finally uncovered the child's face and her expression changed, he put his arm around her shoulders to comfort and support her. The first sign that anything was wrong could be seen in her eyes as they suddenly widened and her expression became one of incredulity.

She did not move, did not take her eyes from that of her child and apart from a sudden sharp intake of breath not a sound could be heard.

In contrast to how slowly the spell had engulfed her, it was suddenly shattered as the child began to cry.

As it did so a tear formed in the corner of her eye.

It ran down her cheek and she shuddered as one does when experiencing that feeling of someone walking on their grave. It was like a cold and indeterminate wind passing through her body..

George wasn't even aware of Len who had come into the room at the sound of them falling to the floor. Len was immobilized, rooted at the sight of the huge man squeezing the life out of his boss. For a second too, his disliking for George Baxter surfaced and he unconsciously felt a moment's pleasure at seeing him punished for all the times he had treated Len with contempt, ordering him about, do this, do that!

Treating him like a dog, someone to wipe his boots on.

Then he did react, grasping Jonas from behind he placed his arm around the man's neck and pulled.

Nothing happened, the gurgling sound was still coming from George, the incoherent cries from Jonas who was trying to strangle him. Len turned to look for something and saw a brown Buddha statue on Jonas' desk. Without considering the possible spiritual implications he grasped the heavy object in both hands and brought it down on the back of Jonas's head. There was a dull thud and Jonas collapsed beneath him. The gurgling noise had stopped, George's eyes seemed to be fixed on some spot on the ceiling. With difficulty, Len managed to drag the inert body from on top of his boss.

He then immediately bent down to see what he could do for George. He quickly loosened his clothing and with his ear to his chest checked his breathing.

There was nothing.

In a state of shock he tried first of all to resuscitate him but in his vain attempts he was unaware that Jonas's final savage attack had crushed his second and third vertebrae. Although trained in first aid, he didn't have the knowledge to recognise the mist that exuded from George's open mouth and nostrils was the release of spinal fluid as a result of the injury.

He would never know that George had died while he had hesitated, that his neck was being crushed just at the moment he had stood there, allowing George to be punished on his behalf. That if he had acted immediately he would have saved his life.

In panic he rushed down the corridor to the laboratory and shouted for Judy's doctor. He saw the man watching Judy who held her baby in her arms. Even if he hadn't been in such a state of panic he wouldn't have understood the emotion that she displayed in her eyes and how incongruous it was in the circumstances. The doctor turned when he heard Len yelling and half ran, was half dragged back down the corridor to Jonas' office. He reacted quickly to the scene before him, attending first of all to Jonas. Blood was trickling down his nearly bald scalp from the wound inflicted by the peaceful Buddha but Jonas' snoring attested to the fact that he had survived the blow. He was quickly pulled away.

"Forget him. Its George!" Len yelled.

The doctor immediately realised that the man had suffered a broken neck and was dead. Nevertheless he went through the motions of checking vital signs and attempting to stimulate the heart. He didn't give it long, it was obvious that the man couldn't be saved. The doctor stood up slowly and looked at Len who also realised the implications.

"I'm sorry," he said quietly.

"That's ok, " said Len suddenly adopting an air of authority. "You can leave now, I'll see to this mess. Get back to your other patient."

The doctor left and Len was alone once more except for the prone bodies of the two men. He looked down at Jonas' corpulent frame and kicked him spitefully in the ribs. An unconscious groan came in response and confirmed that he wouldn't be any trouble for some time. He pulled some handcuffs from a pocket and knelt on Jonas's back while he applied them. He then looked at George and a smirk appeared on his face. He felt different. Suddenly everything had changed. He felt in control as he walked around the desk to make the necessary calls to get the mess cleared up. First of all though he sat in the deep leather chair and allowed himself a moment to get accustomed to his new, if temporary role.

He lifted his feet onto the desk and helped himself to one of Jonas's huge cigars. After rolling it around between his fingers and sniffing the tobacco appreciatively, he bit the end off and spat it out on the floor. Then he lit the cigar and inhaled the rich smoke deeply. He lay his head back and closed his eyes before exhaling rings of blue smoke that drifted slowly towards the air conditioning vent.

He felt quite pleased with himself.

The doctor put his arm around her in order to comfort her and share her sorrow and could not have been blamed for misinterpreting her emotions. The tears she shed were certainly not of sorrow, but of joy as she was engulfed in feelings of relief and love. She gazed intently at the beautiful baby, its little face a mirror of Michael's handsome features. And something much more than mere physical similarity shone within the sparkling eyes. She recognised not just hereditary qualities that were Michael's, but a physical and congenital sameness seemed to exist that went beyond mere inherited similarity.

This was Michael.

The magic of the moment was broken by Len's excited entry and she was taken aback as the policeman dragged the doctor from the room. Then as peace returned again she became oblivious once more to the outside world. She unwrapped her baby and held its face close to hers as she showered its tiny nose and cheeks and lips with gentle kisses. Tears

STILLBORN

continued to roll down her face but they were tears of happiness not sorrow and through them glistened eyes that reflected the joy that she now felt in her heart.

After a while the feelings she had released subsided and she was brought back to reality by the plaintive little cries that came from the tiny rosebud mouth. She looked down into the wrinkled little face and smiled.

She undid her nightdress and let it drop from her shoulders. Tentatively she brought the baby's mouth to her breast and as it closed its little lips eagerly around her nipple she felt an enormous weight fall from her shoulders. She rocked the baby gently as it drank, unconsciously humming a lullaby as much to herself as to her baby. Then in a quiet little voice that was somehow filled with the joy she felt, she tried its name upon her lips, calling to it as she rocked.

"Michael, my little Michael."

The baby looked at her and behind the mist filled blue she thought she saw something in the child's expression.

Recognition.

CHAPTER SEVENTEEN

Judy's baby was taken away while the nurses prepared to remove the afterbirth. Soon after the delivery Judy had been given a drug to induce contraction of her uterus.

Although protected from the pain, she could feel the muscle spasms and could see the nurses working to remove the placenta which for some reason was more difficult than usual.

It was happening at last, the path was finally clear for his arrival into the world. He had worked out from the way in which the contractions had built up to a pitch and then temporarily subsided that his brother had been born. Being the second of twins subjected a baby to more trauma than with a single birth. The period of labour which had been necessary for the birth of his brother had taken its toll from David's strength.

Now, at last it was David's turn.

The contractions had been increasing in strength for some time now and once again he was experiencing that feeling of being pushed down the birth canal through Judy's pelvis and out into the world. He was tired, exhausted by the subjective struggle his little body had endured and he was, not unreasonably, afraid. The muscles tightened around him in an almost vice like grip and he felt his head being forced into the small opening that had been created in Judy's dislocated pelvis. Suddenly the pain was unbearable, his head was filled with flashing lights and he could literally feel his soft and partly formed skull compress. He expected the pain to subside but was terrified when it did just the reverse. The pressure on his brain intensified. Surely I can't get through there, he thought but still he was being pushed deeper. The ligaments on her pelvic joints stretched, the bones of his skull were compressed, he felt complete and utter panic. His heartbeat was amplified in his ears as it was conducted through the bone that closed around him.

Every now and then she would stop pushing and the pain would subside only to begin its ascendancy once again when the next contraction began. His heartbeat faltered, missed a few beats then stopped completely. As the contractions subsided it picked up again, fluttering wildly.

In a moment of clarity he felt he understood at least one reason why consciousness had not been sustained by nature through this process. He cursed himself for having gone against the basic rules of life, his tiny lips stretched over toothless gums in a grimace of agony and perhaps he just imagined his own screams. In those final moments before his birth David would have gladly surrendered his life in exchange for a release from the pain.

His dreams forgotten, the experiment abandoned, his love for Judy sacrificed....anything for release from the pain.

'I'm sorry,' screamed the reincarnate agnostic scientist. 'Please God, please merciful God forgive me...let me die.'

A white light scorched his spirit and in those last moments before his release he once again stood on the threshold between life and death. The stark reality of his mortal experiences was recounted.

Birth itself, he realised, took you through the threshold of death but unlike the previous time he had begun this journey, it did not end in death - this was indeed the other end of the spectrum of life. The two were indivisible. Life was just a circle. Death was life, life was death.

Then it began to subside, both pain and reality. He may have considered that the very pain of his delivery was creating a barrier to his senses in the form of oblivion but he did not find oblivion, he did not find the companion that was unconsciousness and which would envelope him, guide him through this agony and so bring him unscathed into his new life ahead. The labour took much longer than it should have done and by the time he emerged into the world, David was very, very tired, his frail body had been subjected to many hours of strain. Then suddenly it was over, he was forced through the birth canal in one agonising moment when it felt as if the pressure around his head would crush him.

He lost consciousness.

His head was forced out into the air.

Moments later his body followed, still covered in its mucus sack. Limply his little body lay there awaiting the first breath of life.

Hands reached for him, lifting him up to encourage life into him. His eyes, partly open, recorded hazy images.

In the milliseconds that passed before his first breath the reality of what he saw burned deep into his soul. He felt his chest convulse but he choked off that first inward breath. Then he slipped into oblivion.

In the outer laboratory where David and Michael had

STILLBORN

worked for long hours on their early transfer experiments involving primates, a South American chimpanzee went through a solitary labour within the wire mesh walls of her cage. In the early hours of the same day on which Judy also gave birth, the primate too produced her offspring, the first being a healthy male.

The second of her young was born after a difficult and unaided delivery and didn't breath when born.

Instinctively the mother held it close to her breast and patted it with a hairy hand, hoping to encourage life into the tiny body. She lifted it up in front of her face to look at it more carefully.

Its eyes flickered open and its chest began to rise. She didn't recognise the look of fear and horror that appeared on its tiny face when it saw her for the first time.

Suddenly it jerked, its eyes closed and its body went limp. She soon realised that unfortunately this one, also a male, was not going to live. She tossed its limp little body into a corner of the cage and from then on ignored it as she nursed the healthy one.

Later that morning two laboratory technicians carried out their daily work, checking the progress of on-going animal tests, seeing to the welfare of the animals in their cages.

One of them noticed that the chimpanzee had given birth and that one of its young did not seem to be moving.

He reached in to the cage and grasped the limp body, its mother stared at him showing little interest as she fed its healthy twin.

He called to his colleague.

"Eve delivered. Two this time, both males. One seems quite healthy."

"What about the other?"

"No it didn't make it....it's stillborn."

After a cursory inspection he walked over to the incinerator and opening the door placed the small body on the iron grate. Closing the handles firmly, he then ignited the gas.

If the technician had any reason to do so he may have looked more closely at the primitive little face and noticed that its lips were drawn back from its gums in a toothless grimace of fear. Also if he had suspected it, he may have seen a resemblance in its features to Professor David Hawkin.

THE END

The Grave Diggers

By David Mercer

When old Tom finished work
he went to the shed to change his boots.
As he sat alone in the dark, he heard a noise
from where the coffins were stacked up
against the wall.

The noise grew louder and much against
his better judgement, old Tom used a crow-
bar to prise the lid from the offending coffin.

A woman sat up and said.

"Where am I?"

Dr. James Mason investigates and discovers
the woman had died two years earlier.

As the mystery unfolds, the story leaks
out into the newspapers. Within hours there
is widespread panic as people set about
digging up their loved ones who passed
away in similar circumstances.

Just in case they are alive too.

Screaming Souls

By David Mercer

Mary wakes up in a strange place.
It is cold and dark and there are rats
running around the floor.

Gone is her twentieth century
lifestyle and the man she loves.
Instead she finds herself in a
Lunatic Asylum in 1825.

She struggles to hold on to a fading reality
as she is subjected to the horrors of
a not too distant past.

We suffer the cruelty, pain and degradation
with her and when she hides away in her
memories of that other life,
we are there too.

Finally we reach the point when Mary
of today and the child in the Asylum come
face to face.

The question that comes to mind is:
Which one really is Mary?

JORDANIS

By David Mercer

Following the insanity of global nuclear con-
flict, man and beast have perished.

Only computers remain to preside
over a sterile world until even they start to
grind to a halt as their nuclear power
supplies begin to fail.

In a bid to protect itself, the world's most
advanced computer system, Scholar,
needs the help of man.

Scholar clones Jordanis and Angel
from cryogenically stored tissue and rears
them in innocence of their origins.

Unexpectedly Scholar goes 'off-line'.
Jordanis and Angel are on their own.

This story deals with the children's
fight to survive in a world where they seem
to be the only living creatures.

There is of course, a twist in the 'tale'.

The Author:

David Mercer was born in Hampshire in 1945 and
brought up in London.
He has lived a roller coaster life having twice become
a millionaire and just as easily losing it again.
David has experienced over thirty jobs & businesses,
from labourer to engineer, from grave-digger to Time-
share developer, from cheese maker to Estate Agent .
He has lived, worked and travelled in many countries.
Two marriages and several children later, David became a victim of the recession and stripped of his wealth
and family found himself alone with his dog Bruno
and a word processor.
At fifty he has found an outlet for his skills and desires
in writing. His motivation is spiritual, the stories were
waiting to be told, he is merely the instrument.

252